HIDDEN FOLK

BOOKS BY ELEANOR ARNASON

NOVELS

The Sword Smith
To the Resurrection Station
Daughter of the Bear King
A Woman of the Iron People
Ring of Swords
Tomb of the Fathers

COLLECTED STORIES

Ordinary People
Mammoths of the Great Plains
Big Mama Stories
Hidden Folk

HIDDEN FOLK
ICELANDIC FANTASIES

Eleanor Arnason

MANY WORLDS PRESS

BOSTON, MASS. • ST. PAUL, MINN. • 2014

HIDDEN FOLK: ICELANDIC FANTASIES

"Glam's Story" first appeared in *Tales of the Unanticipated*, no. 2 (1987).
Copyright © 1987 by Eleanor Arnason. Reprinted with permission.

"Kormak the Lucky" first appeared in *The Magazine of Fantasy Science
Fiction*, July–August 2013. Copyright © 2013 by Eleanor Arnason.
Reprinted with permission.

"My Husband Stein" first appeared, as "My Husband Steinn," in
Asimov's Science Fiction, October–November 2011. Copyright © 2011
by Eleanor Arnason. Reprinted with permission.

BOOK AND COVER DESIGN: John D. Berry
COVER PHOTOGRAPHS: "Rocks," © 2014 by Dennis Letbetter;
"Icelandic box," © 2014 by Aaron Bell

Published by Many Worlds Press
www.manyworldspress.com

ISBN: 978-0-9903934-0-5

FIRST EDITION
1 2 3 4 5 6 7 8 9

For Jon and Sia Arnason
and Bill Henry

CONTENTS

INTRODUCTION

TO BEGIN WITH THE OBVIOUS: Iceland is an island in the North Atlantic, 600 miles west of Norway and 180 miles east of Greenland. Scotland, to the southeast, is 470 miles away. The island sits directly on the Mid-Atlantic Ridge, and magma from the ridge's Iceland hot spot built the island, which is entirely volcanic rock. Iceland is still geologically active. There are geysers and hot springs all over the island, and the island has a volcanic eruption every few years.

Norse seafarers discovered the island in the ninth century. At the time, it was uninhabited, though Ari the Learned says in his *Book of the Icelanders*, which was written in the early twelfth century, that there were a few Irish monks. According to Ari, they left because they didn't want to live with heathens.

Once discovered by the Norse, the island was rapidly settled, the settlers coming mostly from Norway and Viking settlements in the British Isles. As a result, the people are a mixture of Scandinavian and Gaelic. The culture, however, was almost entirely Norwegian. The only Gaelic residue I know of is certain proper names, such as Njal (Niall) and Kormak (Cormac). The settlers established a republic dominated by large landowners, which lasted until conflicts among landowners in the thirteenth century led to civil war and the collapse of the republic. The island then came under Norwegian rule. It remained a colony of Norway and then Denmark until the twentieth century.

Before settlement about a quarter of the island was covered with forests of birch, willow, and rowan. The remaining land was grassland, marsh, and — in the highlands — rock and ice. The only native mammal was the arctic fox, but there were plenty of birds and rich fishing off the coast. The foxes, birds, and rich fishing remain today.

If the sagas are any indication, life in Iceland was not bad during the first few centuries. The island was connected to Europe and the British Isles by Viking sea routes. Wealthy Icelanders had their own ships, though the number of ship-owning Icelanders decreased over time, till only two are known in the thirteenth century. The Icelanders raised live-stock and exported wool cloth. Especially in the early days, it was possible for a man to hire onto a trading ship or become a mercenary soldier in the British Isles (as Egil Skallagrimsson and his brother did) or go a-viking.

In 1000 CE Iceland was converted to Christianity. As far as I know, the written language of northern pagans — the runic alphabet — was intended for magic, inscriptions, and graffiti, not for extended texts. There was an oral tradition in Iceland, evidenced by surviving skaldic and Eddic poems and by his-tories that must have been oral at first. But it was after the island's conversion that Icelanders began writing things down in a big way, and much of what they wrote was in medieval Icelandic, rather than in Latin.

As a result, we have an extensive body of literature — poetry, histories, historical fiction, and fantastic fiction — written in the vernacular language. Nothing comparable exists in the other Nordic countries. When you study Old Norse, the language of the Vikings, you study Icelandic literature and little else.

Life in Iceland deteriorated during the later Middle Ages. The island suffered from deforestation and soil erosion due to the settlers and their livestock. The climate grew colder. The era of Viking seafaring, which had resulted in colonies in Ice-land, Greenland, the Faeroe Islands, and the British Isles, as well as widespread commerce and pillaging, came to an end. (The pillaging was no fun for the people being pillaged, but it was an important source of income for the northern nations.)

When Denmark acquired Norway in the fourteenth century, Iceland found itself ruled by a continental power with very little interest in any of Norway's North Atlantic possessions, which included Iceland, Greenland, the Faeroe Islands, Shetland, Orkney, the Hebrides, and the Isle of Man. The Danish crown actually lost complete track of the Greenland colony and let it die in isolation. The Icelanders survived, as the Greenlanders did not, but descended into centuries of poverty, punctuated by volcanic eruptions, famine, and plague.

They were not completely isolated, in part because the North Atlantic fishery off Iceland's coast attracted fishermen and merchants from England, Germany, and mainland Scandinavia. This kept Iceland in contact with European culture, according to the Icelandic historian Gunnar Karlsson. In addition, some Icelanders did make it to Denmark. To give an example, in the late eighteenth century the national archivist of Denmark was an Icelandic-Danish scholar named Grimur Jonsson Thorkelin. In 1785 he was given a stipend by the Danish crown to travel through the British Isles and "collect and record all the extant Danish and Norwegian Monuments, Deeds, and Documents" that could be found in British collections. Thorkelin happened upon the only existing copy of *Beowulf* in the British Museum. *Beowulf* is, in a sense, a Danish antiquity, since the king that Beowulf helps by killing Grendel is Hrothgar, king of the Danes. Thorkelin hired a copyist to transcribe the entire poem, then made another copy himself. He took the copies back to Denmark, oversaw the publication of the poem in Copenhagen, and was the first translator of the text. Because I tend to think of eighteenth-century Icelanders as isolated farmers, I am a bit amazed by the idea of Thorkelin copying *Beowulf* in the British Museum and publishing a Latin translation. But he did.

Earlier in the eighteenth century, another Icelandic scholar based in Denmark, Arni Magnusson, gathered large numbers of manuscripts — including saga manuscripts — from Iceland. These ended up in the Arnamagnæan Manuscript Collection in Copenhagen. After Iceland became fully independent in 1944, the Icelanders asked that the manuscripts be returned. Many were repatriated to Iceland in the 1970s and are housed at the Arni Magnusson Institute in Reykjavik.

However, most Icelanders were farmers or fishers, who did not travel to Denmark. For them, the period before the twentieth century was hard. But there were always people on the island who were interested in history and literature. Icelanders were making copies of the sagas from the thirteenth century — when most of the famous sagas were written — until 1922, when the farmer and saga copier Magnus Bjornsson died at the age of eighty-six.

This is one source I use in my stories: the Icelandic family sagas, which are historical fiction about the country's settlers and their descendants, and the information about Norse mythology preserved in the *Poetic Edda* and Snorri Sturlason's *Prose Edda*. All this work is medieval, mostly written in the thirteenth century. The sagas are prose, which is unusual for the Middle Ages. They are mostly realistic, though fantastic elements do creep in. (One example is the battle between Grettir Asmundarson and the undead slave Glam in the *Grettis saga*.) I grew up reading the sagas in translation, and I took Old Norse in graduate school, so I have actually read some Icelandic literature in the original. I think it would be fair to say that my fiction — all of it — is influenced by the sagas. I love their clean, laconic style, their sense of humor and irony, their toughness and heroism, their belief — as Njal says in the *Njals saga* — that "the land is built on law, but through lawlessness is laid waste."

The greatest of all the saga heroes (to me) is Grettir Asmundarson. Njal is a lawyer and a negotiator, a man who tries to maintain lawfulness. Grettir is an outlaw, a man who will go his own way at any cost. He is strong, violent, sarcastic, heroic, and willing to die rather than negotiate. He does die in an epic battle on the island of Drangey, fighting on his knees because he is dying of gangrene and unable to stand.

The Icelanders who wrote the sagas in the thirteenth and fourteenth centuries admired his kind of fierce integrity, but they also knew (I think) that Njal was right. Lawlessness destroyed their republic.

The Eddic poems and stories are different from the sagas, but also likable, especially if you like grimness. I grew up on mythology, including Old Norse mythology. Myths make me happy. I don't feel I need to discuss them here. We all know about Odin and Thor, the ice giants, the world tree.

My other source is Icelandic folktales. The first and most famous collection of these was done by Jon Arnason in the nineteenth century, inspired by the example of the Brothers Grimm. They are stories about elves, trolls, ghosts, famous outlaws, how the great scholar Saemund the Wise outwitted the devil. The human characters are mostly farmers, since Iceland was a peasant society. The elves are handsomer and richer than human Icelanders, but nonetheless seem down-to-earth, a peasant's idea of magical beings. The trolls are very down-to-earth: large, powerful, often dangerous, and usually not so bright. I like the trolls a lot.

Because I like happy endings, I will add that life got a lot better for Icelanders in the twentieth century. They are now a highly educated first-world nation, so modern that they had a banking system that blew up in 2008 along with Wall Street and London. Like the rest of us, they are still recovering from that disaster.

———

"Hidden folk" (*huldufolk*) is an Icelandic name for elves. According to a folktale, God paid Adam and Eve a visit. They greeted him and showed him around their house, then presented their children.

"They all look promising," God said. "But are there any more children?"

Eve answered, "No." But she wasn't telling the truth. There were more children. She hadn't had time to wash and comb them, making them presentable, so she hid them.

God said, "What is hidden from me shall be hidden from people."

So those children and their descendants became invisible to ordinary people, though they could become visible if they wanted to. They lived in rocks and mountains. They were — and are — the elves. I have expanded the name to cover trolls and ghosts.

I want to add a personal note, since the reasons why I love Icelandic literature and folklore are personal.

My father's parents, Sveinbjorn Arnason and Maria Bjarnadottir, came from Iceland to Canada as part of a large migration in the late nineteenth century. Times were hard in the homeland, and something like one-fifth of the population left. My grandparents settled in Manitoba, which had a large Icelandic immigrant community. I realized when writing this that I didn't know how the family ended up in the Chicago area. I asked my brother, and he told me the following story:

Our grandfather Sveinbjorn was a poet in the Icelandic language and was fairly well known in the immigrant community. There was an Icelander who was an inventor, a pretty impressive one, who had an electrical business in Chicago. He admired Sveinbjorn's poetry, so he offered him a job —

mostly, my brother said, to have him around to talk to. "A kind of court poet."

I like the idea of my grandfather getting a job because of his poetry. It speaks well of him and of his employer. The employer, Hjortur Thordarson, collected books as well as poets, and his library is the nucleus of the Icelandic collection at the University of Wisconsin. His estate on Rock Island in Wisconsin is now the Rock Island State Park.

My father went to college at Northwestern University in Evanston, Illinois, and then got an MFA at Princeton, the center for art historical studies at the time. After the war, he got a job at the University of Minnesota. I grew up in Minneapolis, which was heavily Scandinavian American at the time. (It is less so now.)

Our house had Icelandic art and Icelandic books, some in translation and some in the original language. My father told stories about the two years he spent in Iceland during World War II, working for the U.S. government, which had recruited everyone it could find who spoke Icelandic.

Iceland was an important Allied naval and air base, key to controlling the North Atlantic. My father's job was with the U.S. Office of War Information. As far as I can figure out, he was supposed to explain to the Icelanders how their small, isolated country had ended up in a world war. The job was somewhat amorphous, so my father reverted to what he knew — art history — and lectured to the Icelanders in Icelandic on the history of world art. At the time, Icelandic did not have an art historical vocabulary; one hadn't been needed in a country populated mostly by sheep farmers and fisherfolk. Working with a translator, my father invented one. I don't know if this helped with the war effort.

In any case, he came back from Iceland with art, books, and humorous life-in-wartime stories. Iceland was never invaded and turned out to be a safe place to spend the war, though this wasn't known when he went there.

My brother and I had children's versions of the Norse myths when we were kids, along with *Bullfinch's Mythology* and tales from the Bible. In high school, I began to read Icelandic medieval literature — the sagas and Eddas — in translation. As far back as I can remember, I have liked fantastic fiction: folktales and fairy tales, stories about King Arthur, science fiction, the wonderful Chinese novel *Monkey*, and *The Lord of the Rings*. Iceland, especially medieval Iceland, seemed to fit right in.

I went east to college, then came back to Minnesota for graduate school. My major was art history. However, I managed to get into an Old Norse class. Modern Icelandic was not offered, but the two languages are almost identical, except for vocabulary. Modern life and technology have required a lot of new words. I read some medieval Icelandic literature in the original, which was a treat; and I can still read a bit of Old Norse, though I have to keep Zoega's *A Concise Dictionary of Old Icelandic* close at hand.

I wrote the first story in this collection in the 1970s. The rest are more recent, written in the past ten years, after I had been to Iceland twice. It helps to be able to visualize the landscape, which is extraordinary: black mountains, green fields of grass, dark fields of volcanic rock. There are oddly shaped islands off the coast that were trolls until sunlight hit them and they turned to stone.

I visited the island of Drangey — sheer and full of birds — where Grettir made his last stand. As far as I know, Drangey was never a troll. However, long after Grettir died there, it suffered from an infestation of trolls. There is a famous folktale about how Bishop Gudmund the Good blessed the island's cliffs and drove the trolls out. He left one section of cliff unblessed, after a voice spoke out of the rock, saying, "Even the wicked need a place to live." That made sense to the bishop. To this day, an Icelander told me, that section of cliff is unlucky.

I never know how serious the Icelanders are when they tell these stories. They are good stories and worth telling, and they keep the landscape alive. Of course the landscape *is* alive, full of hot springs and geysers and volcanoes that are only resting, getting ready for their next eruption. Why not add trolls and elves? The Icelanders know the rock beneath their feet is full of life.

One final personal note: I am not an expert on Iceland or Icelandic literature. Scholars and ordinary Icelanders know far more than I do. My father knew far more than I do. Rather, I am a fan of Iceland and its literature. These stories are written out of affection and for fun. If you want to know the real Iceland, go there, and read the sagas and modern Icelandic books. People always speak better for themselves. ·

THE SPELLING OF ICELANDIC NAMES

Icelandic has accent marks and several letters, such as the *eth* (ð) and *thorn* (Þ), that are not in modern English, though they were in Anglo-Saxon. I have decided to use English forms of the Icelandic names, rather than deal with the extra orthography.

In addition, Icelandic nouns — including proper names and place names — have four cases: nominative, dative, accusative, and genitive. The nominative is used when a word is the subject of the sentence. The other three cases depend on the pronoun that precedes the noun. In addition, the genitive is also the possessive. My last name — Arnason — is the genitive form of the male weak noun *Arni* plus *son*. It translates to "Arni's son." Arni was my great-grandfather, and my grandfather Sveinbjorn was his son.

Modern Icelanders writing in English use the nominative form of their names. I have decided not to do this. Instead I follow the saga translations I grew up with and the habits of many Icelanders migrating to North America in the nineteenth century and the early twentieth. Weak nouns keep their nominative endings: *i* for male names and *a* for female names. But strong noun names often lose their nominative case endings. Egill becomes Egil; Steinn becomes Stein; Kormakur becomes Kormak.

I am not consistent. I have given my father's name and Hjortur Thordarson's name in the nominative; and, after much thought and going back and forth, I have put the names in "The Black School" in the nominative. I think Saemundur sounds better than Saemund. •

HIDDEN FOLK

GLAM'S STORY

WHEN I MARRIED Thorhall Grimsson, he was a fine-looking fellow, just back from a trading trip and full of stories about the king's court in Norway. He wasn't a wealthy man. His father was given to composing bad poetry, a vice common here in Iceland, and had neglected his farmwork to sit by the fire making up verses. Whenever there was an assembly, you would find old Grim there, reciting his verses in a loud, flat voice to whoever would listen or engaging in verse-making contests with his cronies. He even made a verse for me, shortly after Thorhall and I were married, all full of stuff about broach-goddesses and linen-decked ladies. When Thorhall found out about that, it put him in a foul temper. He stamped around the house, saying that the district would really have something to talk about if anyone found out Grim was making up love poems for his daughter-in-law; and he knew what they would be saying, too, about what was going on at Thorhallsstad.

Poor old Grim sat and scratched his head. He had only been trying to impress me with what a fine poet he was, a fit companion for kings and so on. I told Thorhall he was making a big fuss over nothing. Grim had been talking, not doing; and words have little power for either harm or good. But that is something few Icelanders are willing to believe, since we are richer in words than anything else here in Iceland.

I knew when I married Thorhall that he wasn't going to inherit much except a ramshackle farm and his father's verses, if he cared to remember them. But he seemed to me to be a promising fellow, and I had heard plenty of stories about men making their fortunes trading or raiding in England or Ireland.

Besides, he was tall and broad through the chest and had white blond hair and bright blue eyes. He looked the way I thought Sigurd Fafnisbane would look, or one of King Hrolf Kraki's champions.

The long and short of it was that Thorhall was one of those people who promise much and perform little. He married me and took me to Thorhallsstad. There we stayed, except when there was an assembly to go to. Then Thorhall would get out the clothes he had worn in the king's court in Norway. He would look them over and tell me I must be doing something wrong when I washed the clothes, since they were fading too quickly. He said as well that I wasn't much of seamstress, since everyone could see where I had darned the clothes. Then off we'd go to the assembly, Grim to recite his poetry and Thorhall to walk around in his court finery and discuss politics with his friends. As for me, I visited with my mother and father and brother Bodvar, if he was in Iceland and at the assembly. I had always liked him best of my brothers, though he was always quieter and slower than the rest of them. When he grew up, Bodvar turned into a great traveler. He even got to Russia, which is something few Icelanders do. When his hair began to turn gray, he went to Greenland to settle, saying Iceland had gotten too full of people. I didn't see him after that.

When the assembly was over, Thorhall and Grim and I would go back to Thorhallsstad, which was off by itself in a little valley. There was a waterfall at one end of the valley. A river ran through the valley's bottom, so the land there was marshy. The valley walls were high. We couldn't see out, either northward toward the sea or southward toward the mountains.

Thorhall had only one slave, who stayed home and took care of the farm when we were away. His name was Glam. He was a big fellow and very strong with black hair, a pale face, and dark blue eyes. His mother had been Irish. She told him that she had been a great lady in Ireland, before the Norsemen carried her off. As everyone knows, most of the people who settled in Iceland came from either Norway or Ireland. The settlers from Norway told their children they were Norwegian aristocrats, who left their homeland when Harald Halfdansson became king, for then, they said, they were no longer able to run their lives the way they wanted to, but had to pay attention to King Harald's wishes, and this they refused to do. The settlers from Ireland told their children they were the sons and daughters of Irish kings, whom the Norsemen had captured and carried away from their fine halls to huts in Iceland. As can be seen from this, we in Iceland are the most noble people in the world, since all our ancestors without exception were kings or aristocrats.

Glam's mother told him stories about Christ, so he became a follower of Christ before most other Icelanders. He wore a cross, which he had made from a piece of birch wood, around his neck. He kept the cross out of sight under his shirt and told no one except me whom it was that he prayed to. He said his mother had told him it was no use talking to Norsemen about religion. All the apostles preaching together wouldn't be able to convert one of us. He also said his mother had told him that in her opinion God had created Norsemen to make sure the devil wouldn't be shorthanded, come Judgment Day. He'd have a lot of work then, carrying the damned off to hell, and who would be better helpers than Norsemen? They had carried harmless children off into slavery, unmoved by their pleas. So they hardly would be bothered by the weeping of sinners, found guilty by God.

Most of the time Glam was quiet, but once in a while, when both Thorhall and Grim were out of the house, he would talk to me. He had a deep voice and talked slowly. Often he stopped in the middle of sentences, as if he'd forgotten what he was going to say next. Mostly he talked about his mother and about Ireland. He told me some of the stories she'd told him about the Irish heroes and holy men. He liked hearing the stories Bodvar had told me about the lands around the Baltic Sea and along the great rivers of Russia.

For several weeks after we came back from an assembly, Grim would recite and re-recite the poems he'd composed and make comments about his friends' poetry, most of them unfavorable. Thorhall would tell us all the latest news from Norway, England, Ireland, and Orkney and the doings of the great men of Iceland. He would shake his head over the foolish mistakes made by this chieftain or that one, then tell us what he would have done in the same situation. Glam listened without speaking. Sometimes, when the two of them were looking away from him, he would grin.

Thorhall said later that Glam and I had had closer dealings than we should have, and that's why he killed Glam. But that was a lie. I liked Glam's stories about Ireland, though I didn't believe them. The Irish seem to be terrible liars. Also, he was good with his hands and mended things for me, which Thorhall and Grim left broken, being too busy with politics and poetry. I was grateful for his help. But all we did was talk. Still, as I've said before, it sometimes seems that words count for as much as deeds here in Iceland.

My own opinion is that Thorhall killed Glam because he caught him laughing at one of his speeches about politics, and he made up the story about Glam and me later, when my father asked for my dowry back. By the time he killed Glam, everyone could see that nothing much could be expected of Thorhall. He was going to spend his life on his father's farm, getting poorer rather than richer, for he was as bad a farmer as old Grim. At the assemblies he would watch the great men of Iceland go by in their fine clothes, surrounded by their followers, and he'd listen to men like Bodvar talk about their travels and what this or that foreign king was like. He'd get together with his cronies, and they would talk about the foreign news and give their opinions on what this or that chieftain was doing, not a one of them knowing what he was talking about, since chieftains don't tell their plans to poor farmers. How could a man like this bear to have a slave laugh at him?

Whatever the reason, one night Thorhall came in with blood on his pants and on his right shirtsleeve. His face was paler than usual. He looked sick. My brother Bodvar told me once that it's harder to kill a man than you would think from hearing the stories about Sigurd and King Hrolf Kraki, and that many men feel sick the first few times they do it.

Thorhall said to me, "Glam must've been a Christian man."

I knew as soon as he said that that he'd killed Glam. I said, "What makes you say so, husband?"

"Because he said 'Christ avenge me' when I struck him down."

Old Grim looked up. "You've killed Glam? What did you do that for? Now who will watch the farm when we go to assemblies?"

"I had my own reasons for doing it," Thorhall said, and sat down to eat supper.

Grim scratched his head and sighed. But he asked no more questions, since it was plain that Thorhall was in no mood to answer them.

I don't know what Thorhall did with Glam's body. Wherever he put it, it didn't stay there, as everyone knows who has heard the story of Grettir and Glam. The same night, after we had gone to bed, we heard a noise overhead. At first we thought it was one of the goats, gone up on the roof to graze. Then the whole house began to lunge and twist like a stallion in a horse fight. It seemed unlikely that it would hold together long.

We all ran out the door. Outside the night was still, and a full
moon shone. We looked at the roof. Thorhall said something
I didn't understand. Glam was on the roof, astride the roof's
peak, riding the house as if it were a horse. His face, which had
been pale before, was now as white as new snow, and his dark
eyes were like black holes. Old Grim began to shake. So did
Thorhall. I was less afraid. Glam had done me no harm when
he was alive. Why should he now, when he was dead? Besides,
I was guiltless in the matter of his death. Glam turned his head
and looked at us. Now his eyes shone in the moonlight. I have
never seen a man's eyes shine more brightly. It was hard for me
to meet that gaze, though I had done Glam no harm. Thorhall
grabbed my arm and pulled me after him back into the house.
Grim hurried after us. Once we were back inside, the two of
them barred the door.

My brother Bodvar told me once that some men become so
excited in battle, either from rage or from fear, that they lose
all judgment and run toward the worst danger. Something like
that must have happened to Thorhall to make him flee back
into the house he'd fled out of. I think it was more likely fear
than rage that made him run toward danger.

There we stayed for the rest of the night, with the house
rocking and creaking around us, and Thorhall and Grim both
shaking. I can't say I was entirely fearless then, since it seemed
likely the house would fall down on top of us. But Thorhall
wouldn't let me go outside. As it turned out, the house stayed
in one piece, though the roof beams cracked and sagged. Toward morning, Glam climbed down off the roof and went elsewhere. The house stopped shaking. When that happened, we
packed up our belongings as quickly as we were able. When
morning came we left the house and the valley and went to
the nearest neighbor's house.

The man who lived there was named Kalf. He was a cousin

of Grim's, a small, thin fellow with sharp black eyes and a big lower lip, which he tugged when he was thinking. Thorhall told him that Glam had been killed in a fall, going up one of the valley's walls after a sheep, and then had come back to haunt us. "Though I don't know why he would do this," Thorhall said.

Kalf frowned and tugged his lip and told Thorhall he didn't know either. "But it's typical of you, Thorhall, to be bothered by ghosts when nobody else is." Then he told us we had better stay at his house till something was done about Glam.

In the afternoon, Thorhall went off to see how our livestock were doing. He wasn't gone long. When he came back his face was pale. He said he'd seen Glam walking around the valley in broad daylight. When Kalf heard this, he tugged his lip again, then said, "It seems to me the best thing for you to do is hire a fellow to watch your livestock. I have a man here I'd just as soon get rid of, because he eats too much. But he's big and strong and afraid of nothing."

As everyone knows who knows the story of Grettir and Glam, the man was named Thorgaut. He was a big fellow with gray hair and gray eyes and a broad, flat, ugly face. He was from Borgarfjord. He had left there because the family at Borg let no one get ahead except their own relatives, or so he said. "I came here to see if the great men in this part of Iceland were any fairer than those in Borgarfjord," he said. "But I can see already it's just as hard for a poor man to get ahead here, unless he's lucky enough to have powerful relatives."

Thorhall told him about Glam. Kalf said his advice to Thorgaut was that he take Thorhall's job.

Thorgaut looked at Kalf, then frowned. "It seems to me, if I'm going to work at all, it's going to be for Thorhall."

"That may be," Kalf said. "I have heard a lot of the champions in the old days were big eaters, but I'm not rich the way

King Hrolf was. I can't afford to keep a man who eats the way you do. Besides, I don't need a champion."

Thorgaut said, "A poor man must take whatever work he can find. I'll take care of your livestock for you, Thorhall."

The next morning Thorgaut set off for Thorhallsstad, and that was the last I ever saw of him.

After he had been gone for a week, Thorhall and Kalf went to see what had happened to him. When they came back, they looked grim. Kalf said they had found Thorgaut close by our farmhouse, lying dead in the grass, his neck broken. "Glam must have gotten him," Kalf said.

I said that sounded unlikely to me, since Glam had always been a peaceful man.

"Death is a great changer," Kalf said. "It isn't surprising that Glam isn't the same man he used to be."

I didn't say anything more. Kalf was a man who didn't like people disagreeing with him, especially women. But I thought and still think that Thorgaut must have gotten frightened when he met Glam and run away and tripped and fallen, breaking his neck.

Thorhall said they had buried Thorgaut where they found him, then left quickly, for they saw Glam coming toward them down one of the valley slopes.

After that, things stayed the way they were for some time. We stayed at Kalf's house. At first he was glad to have us, since his wife was dead, and he had no one to see to the cooking and housecleaning. But after several weeks he began to mutter that he'd made a poor trade, exchanging Thorgaut for three people, all of them hearty eaters. Every time someone stopped at his farm, Kalf asked him if he knew anyone willing to help Thorhall get rid of Glam. But by this time the district was full of stories about Glam, and no one was willing to meet him. Kalf grew more and more foul tempered. He glowered at Grim if the old fellow tried to recite one of his poems, and he told Thorhall that poor men who had to eat other men's food had no right to political opinions.

At this point a new person comes into my story, a fellow everyone must have heard of, since they tell stories about Grettir Asmundarson in every part of Iceland. Many people say he's the greatest man who has lived in Iceland up till now, or at least the greatest outlaw. He lived in Iceland as an outlaw for fifteen years, which is longer than any other outlaw has lasted. Furthermore, people say, he would have lasted longer if he hadn't wounded himself by accident and been too sick to fight off the men who came after him. It was typical of Grettir that he died in such a way. He was terribly unlucky.

Grettir's fight with Glam took place before he was outlawed. Many people say Glam cursed him during the fight, and it was because of this curse that Grettir's luck turned bad, and he became an outlaw. But I don't know if this story is true or false.

He came to Kalf's house late one afternoon. I was the first person to meet him. Thorhall was out helping Kalf with some kind of farmwork, and old Grim was asleep by the fire.

Grettir was eighteen or nineteen years old at that time, a big man with a broad face covered with freckles. His hair was red. His beard, which was short and sparse, was red too, though not the same shade of red. He had thick eyebrows, which were sun-bleached blond, and dull blue eyes. Most of the time when I was around him, he was restless and fidgety, always doing something like scraping his teeth clean with a thumbnail or chewing on a fingernail or scratching some part of his head. Thorhall was with Grettir when he fought Glam. He said that Grettir stopped being restless as soon as he heard Glam coming, and he waited without moving until it was time to fight.

I greeted Grettir and asked him what his business was. He told me he had come to take care of Glam.

"That may prove difficult," I said. I asked him his name.

He said he was Grettir Asmundarson. Though he became more famous later, Grettir was already well known. I looked at him again. When I knew who he was, I noticed how broad his chest was and how thick his neck. Then I saw his big hands with knobby knuckles. His fingernails were bitten short, and the cuticles were torn. He had his helmet on his head and his shield on his arm. His famous single-edged sword was at his side. All in all, he looked ready to take on anyone.

"It may be that you'll be able to deal with Glam, Grettir, though I doubt it," I said. "Maybe you'd be better off if you went home."

Grettir grinned briefly. "Harm can come to a man even sitting by his own hearth, as your husband has found, Goodwife Gudrun."

It was plain that he was going to go after Glam no matter what I said, so I made him welcome. Old Grim woke when Grettir came in. He greeted him and made up a verse when he learned who Grettir was. I didn't listen, for just then I saw a bone under the table. It was a big, white thighbone that must have come from Kalf's old cow. We had been eating her for the past week. I bent and picked up the bone. There were tooth marks on it. Kalf's dog had been chewing on it, trying to crack it open.

Grettir recited a verse of his own in answer to Grim's verse. It sometimes seems to me that every Icelander who isn't either dumb or half-witted makes up poetry, and most of it terrible. Grim perked up and came back with another verse. I hadn't seen him so happy since the last assembly. I went to fix supper. Grettir was frowning and biting his thumbnail while he put together a new verse. They were still at it when Kalf and Thorhall came in. Kalf frowned. "What's wrong with you, Gudrun? Isn't one hungry poet enough? Did you have to go and get another one?"

Grettir turned red and stood up. I said quickly, "Kalf, this is Grettir Asmundarson. He's come to help get rid of Glam."

Kalf turned pale when he heard Grettir's name. It is never a good idea to insult a hero, and Grettir had a reputation for being hot tempered and more than ready to test his strength against the strength of others. Kalf said it was an honor to have a hero like Grettir in his house, and his help would be appreciated, since no ordinary man could deal with Glam. "Or even a man like Thorgaut, who was bigger and stronger than average and fearless, too. But I've heard how you did in those berserkers in Norway. It seems to me you ought to be able to handle Glam."

Grettir grinned then. When he smiled, it was always briefly, and he didn't look happy when he smiled.

We ate supper. While we ate, Thorhall told Grettir about Glam. He told the same story he'd told Kalf, saying Glam had been killed in an accident. Grettir frowned as he listened and rolled bits of bread into hard balls, which he ate. When the story was done, Grettir said he would go up to Thorhallsstad the next day. Thorhall offered to go with him, which surprised me. I think he meant to go back to the valley not to help Grettir but to gather together whatever sheep and cattle he could find and drive them to Kalfsstad. As it was, we had nothing except our clothes and some of our household goods. So long as Glam had our farm and livestock, we were landless paupers. I think that frightened Thorhall more than Glam did.

The long and short of it was that early the next morning Grettir and Thorhall rode off together. They were gone three days. While they were gone, I came closer to quarreling with Kalf than I ever had before. He was in the house more than usual and forever complaining: his food was cold; his clothes hadn't been dried properly; the fire had been badly built; there was a draft coming from somewhere. I think he was afraid that Glam would kill both Grettir and Thorhall, and he'd be stuck with me and old Grim. Grim was silent for once. He looked more and more worried as time went by, but all he did was huddle by the fire. As for me, I was more fidgety than usual and shorter tempered. At night I had trouble sleeping.

The morning of the fourth day, Grettir and Thorhall came back. They were both walking. Grettir seemed very stiff. His clothes were torn to shreds, and there were dark bruises all over his arms and chest. He had a black eye, too. Thorhall looked unharmed, except he was limping. He said he had gotten a sharp stone in his shoe coming back and had cut his foot.

All Grettir said was, "Glam isn't likely to bother you any more." Then he lay down and went to sleep.

We asked Thorhall what had happened. He said they had spent three nights at Thorhallsstad. "It's strange," he said, "but this time we saw no sign of Glam by day, though he was active enough at night."

"That's not so strange," Kalf said. "Glam must have recognized Grettir and thought it wisest to stay away from him during the day. As everyone knows, ghosts aren't as strong when the sun shines as they are after dark."

"That may be," Thorhall answered. Then he told us that on the first night nothing happened except sheep he found and penned were let loose. The second night, Glam broke into the outbuilding where they had put their horses and killed both of the animals. "When that happened, I told Grettir we'd both be safer elsewhere, but he said, 'I'm not losing a horse without getting something in exchange.' So we stayed a third night."

In later times, when Thorhall described the fight between Grettir and Glam, he told how on the third night Glam rode the roof again and kicked it till the rafters cracked, then came down, came inside, and took hold of Grettir. The two of them wrestled around the house, so Thorhall said, and broke all the furniture. Finally Grettir pushed Glam against the top of the door so hard that Glam went through the doorframe and broke the roof above it. The two of them tumbled out into the moonlight. There Grettir pulled out his famous sword and hacked off Glam's head. That is the story Thorhall told for years after at every assembly to everyone who would listen. But the first time he told the story, after he and Grettir came back to Kalfsstad, he said only, "We don't have much to come back to, Gudrun. Grettir and Glam between them have wrecked our house. Glam got his head cut off. Grettir and I burned him and buried the ashes."

After he said that, Thorhall went to sleep. Kalf went out to see to a sick ewe, and Grim settled by the fire to compose a new poem, this one about Grettir and Glam. I went back to my housework.

Grettir and Thorhall slept all day. In the evening, Thorhall woke and ate supper, but Grettir slept on. Finally, when it was late and the house was full of shadows, Grettir began to move restlessly in his sleep. Soon there was sweat on his face. His lips were pressed tightly together, and his hands were clenched. He grew more and more restless, till at last he sat up, opened his eyes, and pulled out his sword, looking around him. We all watched him. His face was pale and shining with sweat. "It's too dark in here. Put more wood on the fire," he said.

I built up the fire. We didn't ask him what he had dreamed. After a while, we went to bed, but Grettir stayed sitting up, his sword in his hand. When I got up in the morning, the fire was still burning, and Grettir was still sitting beside it, his sword in his hand.

He never told us what he had dreamed about. But he told other people, or so I've heard, that he'd seen Glam's eyes shining in the moonlight when they tumbled together out of the dark house, and it was the only sight he'd ever seen that had frightened him. As everyone in Iceland knows, after the fight with Glam, Grettir became afraid of the dark, for it seemed to him that it held horrors that were about to make themselves visible; and he always tried to be with other people when night came.

After breakfast, Grettir went on his way in new clothes that Thorhall gave him, on a horse that Kalf lent him. The clothes were too tight, since Grettir was a bigger man than Thorhall, and the horse was ancient and swaybacked, since Kalf never lent anything that was any use to him. I never saw Grettir again.

As for Thorhall and Grim and me, we went back to Thorhallsstad. The farmhouse was wrecked. Most of our sheep and cattle were lost in the mountains. By this time, I was tired of Thorhall and his politics and his poor husbandry. Besides, with Glam dead, there was no one at Thorhallsstad whom I wanted to talk to. So I went home to my parents. I can't say my father was happy to see me. He said, when he paid my dowry to Thorhall, he had expected I'd be no further expense to him, but here I was back, ready to eat his food again. But my mother said if he didn't want his daughter back, he should have picked a better husband for her.

"How can you expect any girl to stay with a fellow with so little sense that he gets himself haunted?" my mother said. By this time, both my parents had become followers of Christ, so she added, "If Thorhall had been a Christian man, none of this would have happened. Everyone knows that ghosts and trolls fear crosses and holy relics, but Thorhall had none of these around. Though, Christian or pagan, he still would have been a bad farmer, for I've yet to see that changing religions makes idle men industrious or fools wise."

After that, my father said nothing more about my coming home. He tried to get my dowry back from Thorhall, saying it was Thorhall's fault that our marriage had broken up, since he'd more or less driven me out by filling the house with ghosts. But Thorhall said by the time I had left him, Glam was safely underground; and also, he had nothing left except a broken-down house and a few sheep. How could he pay anyone anything? It was at this point that he said that I had treated Glam as if he had been my husband, instead of my husband's slave. By this time, Bodvar had gone to Greenland. My father was getting old, and my other brothers were all peaceful men. So Thorhall didn't get into any trouble from his slanders. The long and short of it was, my father didn't get a penny from him.

I married again several years later, this time to a man who kept quiet most of the time and had no interest in politics. He was a good farmer, though. His name was Kjarval Steinsson, and he was half Irish like Glam, though Kjarval was a free man, the son of a Norwegian who had spent some time in Dublin and gotten married there. Like Glam, Kjarval had been Christian all his life, which was something few Icelanders could say, except those who were small children. We were married by a priest in a church.

Sometimes I saw Thorhall at assemblies, dressed in his threadbare court clothes, talking about politics or about the deeds of Grettir Asmundarson the famous outlaw and retelling the story of Grettir's fight with Glam. When Thorhall saw me, he turned his head and hurried away. But Grim talked to me from time to time. Life was hard at Thorhallsstad, he said. They grew poorer and poorer. All their luck had left them when the haunting began, and it had never come back. There must have been more to Glam than anyone had thought, for he'd taken their luck and Grettir's luck, too, who was the strongest man who had ever lived in Iceland.

Kjarval said to me that it wasn't Glam who'd taken their luck, but rather Christ. Glam's last words had been "Christ avenge me," and that's exactly what Christ had done, or so Kjarval said. He had raised Glam up the way he'd raised Lazarus and sent him to drive Thorhall from his home. When Grettir fought Glam, he had been setting himself against Christ, which is why his luck turned bad. When we heard that Grettir was dead, after living for fifteen years as an outlaw in Iceland's wastes, and that his head had been hacked off with his own sword, the one he'd used to behead Glam, Kjarval said, "You see Christ's power. He has cast down many things in foreign lands, or so the priests say. Here in Iceland, he has brought Grettir the Strong to his end."

If this is right, Grettir got no more than he deserved. What harm had Glam done to anyone except Thorhall, who was his killer? And who can blame a man for avenging his own death? So tell me what cause Grettir had to come and hack off Glam's head and burn Glam to ashes?

I have heard a lot of stories about Grettir. Most of them agree that he was always restless and uneasy, except when he was in serious trouble. Then, when he readied himself to meet whatever blows were about to be dealt him, he was calm. It was this peculiarity, I believe, that sent him from one fight to another with hardly a rest between. Most people seek peace, though they go about it in a lot of different ways. Grettir sought it, too. But he could feel peace only when he was engaged in some great struggle. It's my opinion that Grettir went after Glam not so much to get Glam as to get the moment before the battle, when he lay without moving in the dark house and heard Glam's blows breaking down the bolted door, and maybe also the moment after the battle, when Glam lay dead at his feet. Then Grettir's great strength was exhausted, and he was too tired to feel uneasy.

So Glam died the first time so that Thorhall Grimsson could have a little respect. The second time he died so that Grettir Asmundarson could have a moment or two of peace. It may be that Glam's ghost can take comfort in this, wherever he is now, knowing that he has been useful to his betters.

But it seems to me that a man like Glam was more use to the world than an idle talker like Thorhall or a hero like Grettir, who did much that will be remembered, most of it harmful. For Glam did his work well and lived in peace with the people around him. It seems to me now that the best kind of people are those like Glam and Kjarval, who stay home and stay out of trouble and do the work that is at hand. •

KORMAK THE LUCKY

THERE WAS A MAN named Kormak. He was a native of Ireland, but when he was ten or twelve, Norwegians came to his part of the country and captured him, along with many other people. They were packed into a ship and carried north, along with all the silver the Norwegians could find, most of it from churches: reliquaries and crosses, which they broke into bits, so it could be traded or spent. The Norwegians planned to take their cargo to one of the great market towns, Kaupang in Norway or Hedeby in Denmark. There the Irish folk would be sold as slaves.

The ship left Ireland late and got caught in an autumn storm that blew it off course. Instead of reaching Norway, it made landfall in Iceland, sailing into the harbor at Reykjavik in bad condition. The Norwegians decided it would be too dangerous to continue the journey through stormy weather. Instead they found Icelanders who were willing to host them for the winter. The Irish were sold. They brought less than they would have in Kaupang or Hedeby. However, the Norwegians did not have to house and feed them through the winter.

In this manner, Kormak came to Iceland and became a slave. He was a sturdy boy, sharp-witted and clever with his hands. But he was lazy and curious and easily distracted. This did not make him a good worker. As a result, he was sold and traded from one farmstead to another, going first east, then north and west, and finally back south to Borgarfjord. It took eight years for Kormak to make this journey around Iceland. In this time, he became a tall young man with broad shoulders and rust-red hair. His eyes were green. He had a beard, though it was thin and patchy, and he kept it short when possible. A long scar went down the side of his face, the result of a beating. It pulled at the corner of his mouth, so it seemed that he always had a one-sided, mocking smile.

The next-to-last man who owned him was a farmer named Helgi, who did not like his work habits better than any of Kormak's previous owners. "It's past my ability to get a good day's work out of you," Helgi said. "So I am selling you to the Marsh Men at Borg, and I can tell you for certain you'll be sorry."

"Why?" asked Kormak.

"The master of the house at Borg is named Egil. He's an old man now, but he used to be a famous Viking. He's larger than most human people, ugly as a troll, and still strong, though his sight is mostly gone. The people at Borg are all afraid of him, and so are the neighbors, including me."

"Why?" asked Kormak a second time.

"Egil is bad tempered, avaricious, self-willed, and knows at least some magic, though mostly he has used brute force to get his way. He's also the finest poet in Iceland."

This didn't sound good to Kormak. "You said he's old and mostly blind. How can he rule the household?"

"His son Thorstein does most of the managing. He's an even-tempered man and a good neighbor. He will cross his father if it's a serious matter, but most of the time he leaves the old man alone. If you make Egil angry, he will kill you, in spite of his blindness and age."

Several days later Thorstein Egilsson came down the fjord to claim Kormak. He was middle-aged, fair-haired, and handsome with keen blue eyes. He rode a dun horse with black mane and tail and carried a silver-mounted riding whip. A second horse, a worn-out mare, followed the first. His mount, Kormak thought.

Thorstein paid for Kormak, then told him to mount the mare, which had a bridle, but no saddle. Kormak obeyed.

They rode north. The season was spring, and the fields around them were green. Wild swans nested among the grazing sheep.

After a while, Thorstein said, "Helgi says you are strong, which looks true to me, and intelligent, but also lazy. You have been a slave for many years. You should have learned better habits. I warn you that I expect work from you."

"Yes," replied Kormak.

"I know you can't help your smile," Thorstein added. "But I want no sarcasm from you. There are enough difficult people at my homestead already."

They continued riding up the valley. After a while, Thorstein said, "I have one more thing to tell you. Stay away from my father."

"Why?" asked Kormak, though he was almost certain he knew the answer to this question.

"He used to be a great Viking. Now he's old and blind, and it makes him angry. I plan to use you in the outbuildings away from the hall. It isn't likely you'll meet him. If you do and he asks you to do anything, obey and then get away from him as quickly as you can."

"Very well," said Kormak.

They came over a rise, and he saw the farm at Borg. There was a large long hall, numerous outbuildings, and a home field fenced with stone and wood. Horses and cattle grazed there. Farther out open fields spread across the valley's bottom, dotted with sheep. A river ran past the farm buildings, edged with marshy ground. Everything looked prosperous and well made. It was a better place than any farm he'd known before.

They rode down together, and Thorstein led the way to an outbuilding. A large man stood outside. He was middle-aged with ragged black hair and a thick black beard.

"This is Svart," Thorstein said. "You'll work for him, and he will make sure you do your work."

Svart grunted. This must be agreement.

Thorstein and Kormak dismounted, and Svart took the reins of Thorstein's horse. "Come," he said to Kormak.

They unsaddled Thorstein's mount and rubbed the two animals down, then led them to the marshy river to drink. Kormak's feet sank deep into the mucky ground.

Svart said, "Thorstein is a good farmer and a good householder. But he's firm. Do exactly as he tells you. No back talk and no hiding from work."

"Yes," said Kormak, thinking this might be a difficult place.

They let the horses free in the home field to graze, and Svart began to tell Kormak about the labor he would do.

So began Kormak's stay among the Marsh Men. The family got its nickname from their land, which was marshy in many places. Channels had been cut in the turf to draw water out and carry it to the river. This helped the fields. Nothing could make the riverbanks anything but mucky.

Svart was a slave, but he was good with animals and knew iron smithing. This made him valuable. He was left alone to do his work, which was caring for the farm's horses. Kormak's job was to help him and obey his commands. If he was slow, Svart hit him, either with his hand or with a riding whip. Nonetheless, at day's end they would rest together. Svart would talk about the family at Borg, as well as his travels with Thorstein to other farmsteads and to the great assembly, the Althing, at Thingvellir. The Marsh Men were a strong and respected family. When Thorstein traveled, he wore an embroidered shirt and a cloak fastened with a gold broach. His horse was always handsome. Retainers traveled with him, and Svart came along to care for the animals.

"Everything in his life is well regulated, except for his father," Svart said.

Kormak said nothing, but he thought that the old man could hardly cause much harm. Eighty years old and blind!

He had no reason to visit the long hall, but he'd seen the members of the family at a distance. For the most part, they were handsome people, who wore fine clothing even when they were home. The old man was unlike the rest: tall and gaunt and ugly, his head bald and his beard streaked with white and gray. Thick eyebrows hid his sightless eyes. He felt his way around the farmstead with a staff or guided by one of his daughters.

Svart went on talking. He had spent most of his life at Borg and remembered Egil's father Skallagrim, another big, dark, ugly man with an uncertain temper. Strange as it seemed to Kormak, Svart was proud of the family and interested in what they did. The servants who worked in the long hall told him stories about Thorstein and the rest of the Marsh Men. He repeated these to Kormak.

"Thorstein rarely crosses his father, but he did so recently. The old man has two chests of silver, which he got from the English king Athelstein. Athelstein gave him the silver as compensation for Egil's brother, who died fighting for the king. The money should have gone to Skallagrim, who was still alive then. It was Skallagrim who'd lost a good son, who could have defended him from enemies and supported him in old age. 'Bare is the back with no brother behind him,' and even worse is a back unprotected by sons.

"But Egil kept the chests, because he is avaricious.

"Now that he's old and enjoys little, Egil decided to play a game with the silver. He planned to take it to the Althing, to the Law Rock, which is the most sacred place in Iceland. When he got there, he planned to open the chests and scatter the silver as widely as he could. Of course men would struggle to get it. Egil hoped they would draw weapons and break the Thing Peace, and he hoped that he would be able to hear them fight.

"The old man has always settled problems through violence or magic. But Thorstein is a different person, and he said the old man couldn't break the Thing Peace. 'The land is built on law,' as the saying goes. 'Without law it becomes a wilderness.' Thorstein would not let anyone in his household make a wilderness in Iceland.

"So now the old man is sulking, because he couldn't do the harm he wanted to."

Let him sulk, thought Kormak. What kind of man would plan this kind of harm? Though it was pleasant to think about the prosperous farmers of Iceland fighting over bits of silver.

Svart told this story one day in summer, when the sun rarely left the sky. Then came fall, when the days shortened and the sheep were gathered in, then winter, dark and long. Kormak tended the horses in their barn. In all this time, nothing important happened, either good or bad, though he did become a better worker. He learned that he liked horses and the skills that Svart taught him. He even learned some smithing during the dark winter days.

Spring came again. The sky filled with light, which spilled down over everything, and the wild birds came back to nest. Falcons stole the nestlings, swooping down from the brilliant sky. The farmworkers watched for eagles, which could take a lamb.

One day Egil came to their building, feeling his way with his staff. Close up, he was uglier than at a distance. His nose was wide and flat; his eyes, barely visible under bristling eyebrows, were covered with gray film; his teeth were yellow and broken. A monster, Kormak thought.

"Svart?" Egil called in a harsh voice. "Saddle three horses. I want to ride into the mountains with you and the Irish slave."

Svart looked surprised, then said, "Yes."

They had both been told to obey Egil's commands, but Kormak felt uneasy. Thorstein was away visiting neighbors. They could not go to him. The people left on the farm would not oppose Egil.

What could they do, except what they did?

They saddled the horses with the old man standing near, leaning on his staff and listening. The one picked for Egil was an even-tempered gelding, entirely black except for his mane, which had red hairs mixed with the black. It reminded Kormak of rusty iron. Svart picked another gelding for himself, brown with a light mane and tail. Kormak got a mare that was spotted white and blue-gray. They were all good horses, but Egil's was the best.

When they were done, Svart helped the old man into the saddle, and the two of them mounted.

"To the long hall first," the old man said.

They obeyed and stopped by a sidewall. Two bags lay on the ground. "Get them," Egil said.

Kormak dismounted and put a hand on the first bag. It was so heavy he needed both hands to lift it. Inside the leather was something with edges, a box or chest.

It might have been magic, or maybe the old man had some sight left. He seemed to know what Kormak was doing and said, "Give one bag to Svart and take the other yourself."

Kormak obeyed, heaving one bag up to Svart and then heaving the other onto his mare, which moved a little and nickered softly. He knew what she was saying. "Don't do this."

What choice did he have? He mounted and settled the bag in front of him. Egil carried nothing except his long staff and the sword at his side.

"Go up along the river," Egil said.

They rode, Svart first, leading Egil's horse. Kormak came last. How had the old man been able to move the bags by himself? Had someone helped him, or was he that strong?

A trail went along the river. They followed it, going up over rising land. Around them the spring fields were full of sheep and lambs. Svart kept talking, telling Egil what they were passing. At last the old man told them to turn off the trail. Their horses climbed over stones, among bushes and a few trees, small and bent by the wind. The land had been forested when the settlers came, or so Kormak had been told. But the trees had been cut for firewood, and sheep had eaten the saplings that tried to rise. Now the country was grass and bare rock and — in the mountains — snow and ice.

They came finally to the edge of a narrow, deep ravine. A waterfall rushed down into it, and a stream tumbled at the ravine's bottom, foaming white in the shadow.

"Dismount and help me to dismount," Egil said, his harsh voice angry. This was a man who had needed little help in his life. He had served one king and quarreled with another, driving Eirik the Bloodaxe out of Norway through magic. He'd fought berserkers and saved his life by composing a praise poem for Eirik, when Norway's former king held him captive in York. Now a slave had to give him assistance when he climbed down off a horse.

Kormak knew all of this from Svart. He dismounted, lifted the bag to the ground, and watched as Svart helped Egil down.

"There are chests inside the bags," Egil said. "Take them out and empty them into the waterfall."

Svart moved first, pulling a chest from his bag and opening it. "It's full of silver," he said to Egil.

"I know that, fool!" Egil said. "This is the money Thorstein would not let me spend at the Althing. He's not going to inherit it when I die. Toss it into the ravine!"

Svart took the chest to the ravine's edge and turned it over. Bright silver spilled out, shining briefly in the sunlight before it fell into the ravine's shadow.

"Now you," Egil said, and turned his head toward Kormak. The eyes under his heavy brows were as white as two moons.

Kormak pulled the chest from his bag and carried it to the ravine's edge. Pulling the top up, he spilled the silver — coins and bracelets and broken pieces — into the river below. As he did so, he heard a cry and glanced around. Svart was down. Egil stood above him with a sword. Blood dripped from the blade. Kormak tossed his chest into the river and turned to face the old man, who came at him, swinging his bloody sword. How could he see?

The blade, swinging wildly from side to side, almost touched Kormak. He twisted away, losing his balance, and fell into the ravine, shouting with surprise.

He fell a short distance only, landing on a narrow ledge and scrambling onto his knees. His back hurt, as well as a shoulder and an elbow. But he didn't pay attention to the pain. Instead he looked up. The old man was directly above him, looking down with his blind eyes. "I heard you cry out, Kormak. Did you fall in the river? Or are you hiding? If so, I will find you, either with my staff or magic. I want no one to tell Thorstein what I did with the silver."

Kormak said nothing. After a moment, the old man vanished. Shortly after, Svart's body tumbled off the ravine edge, falling past Kormak. An out-flung hand hit Kormak as the body passed. He almost cried out a second time, but did not. Instead he crouched against the cliff wall, pressing his lips together. Below him, Svart vanished into the river's foam. Cold spray from the waterfall came down on Kormak like fine rain, making the ledge slippery.

The old man reappeared at the ravine's edge. "I can bring stones and roll them down on you. If you haven't joined Svart in the river, you will then."

The old man was trying to trick him into making a noise. Kormak kept his lips pressed together.

Egil knelt clumsily at the cliff rim and pushed his staff down along the stone wall, swinging it back and forth. Kormak lay down on his back, making himself as flat as possible. The staff's tip swung above him, almost touching. Kormak sucked his belly in and tried not to breathe.

"Well, then," the old man said finally. "It will have to be stones. I wish you had been more cooperative. Look at Svart. He gave me no trouble at all."

The old man stood stiffly. Once again he vanished. Kormak sat up. He looked around for an escape. But the cliff wall was sheer. He could see only one way off the ledge: jumping into the turbulent, dangerous river below him. He stood, thinking he would have to risk this.

A short distance away from him, at one end of the ledge, a door opened in the cliff wall. A man looked out. He was tall and even handsomer than Thorstein Egilsson, with long, silver-blond hair that flowed over his shoulders and a neatly trimmed, silver-blond moustache. His shirt was bright red, his pants were dark green, and his belt had a gold buckle. The man smiled and beckoned.

This seemed a better choice than the river. Kormak walked to the door. The man beckoned a second time. Kormak stepped inside, and the man closed the door. They were in a corridor made of stone and lit by lanterns. It extended into the distance, empty except for the two of them.

"Welcome to the land of the elves," the man said. "I am Alfhjalm, a retainer of the local lord."

Kormak gave his name and thanked the elf for saving him from Egil.

"We keep track of the Marsh Men, because they have always been troublesome neighbors," Alfhjalm said. "As a rule, we don't cross them, since we don't want to attract attention. But we have a grudge against Egil, and now that he is old and weak, we are willing to disrupt his plans."

"Will he die out there?" Kormak asked, hoping that Egil would. The old man had killed Svart, who trusted him.

"We don't want Thorstein coming here to bother us, as he certainly will if he can't find his father. He has no magic powers, but he is a persistent man. Some of my companions have gone out to lead the horses away, making enough noise so Egil will be able to follow. In this way, they will lure him out of the mountains and close to home. Then they'll help him catch the horses, so he can ride home with dignity. If they do their job well, he will never know that elves were involved. We like to remain hidden and unknown.

"As for you, come with me."

They walked along the corridor, which went on and on. After a while, Kormak noticed that the lamps cast a strange light, pale and steady, not at all like the light of burning wood or oil. He stopped and looked into a lamp. Inside was a pile of clear stones with sharp edges. The light came from them.

"They are sun stones," the elf said. "If we set them in sunlight, they take the sunlight in and then pour it out like water from a jug, until they are empty and go dark. Then our slaves replace the stones with fresh ones, full of light."

"You have slaves?" Kormak asked.

"We are like Icelanders, except more clever, fortunate, healthy, and prosperous. The Icelanders have slaves, and so do we."

This made Kormak uneasy. But he kept walking beside the elf, who was taller than he was and had a sword at his side.

At last they came to an open space. Light shone from above, though it was dimmer than the spring light in Borgarfjord. Looking up, Kormak saw a dark roof, dotted with many brilliant points of light.

"Are those stars?" he asked.

"No," said the elf. "They are sun stones, like the ones in our lamps. If the stones are solitary, they gradually fade. But we can connect them, laying them one after another through channels in the rock. Then each pours light on the next and renews it. In this way they bring sunlight from the high mountains into our home. They never dim in the summer. But in winter it can be dark here."

Below the sky were high, black cliffs ringing a flat valley. Groves of trees dotted the valley. Animals grazed in green fields. In the middle of all this was a long hall, larger than the one at Borg. The roof shone as if covered with gold.

"That is my lord's hall," Alfhjalm said. "Come and meet him."

They walked down a slope into the valley. The fields around them were full of thick, lush grass. The animals grazing — sheep and cattle and horses — all looked healthy and well fed. Many had young, which meant it was spring in Elfland as well as in Iceland.

Kormak had never seen handsomer horses. They were larger than Icelandic horses and every color: tan, red-brown, dark-brown, black, blue-gray, and white, with black or blond manes. As he and the elf walked past, the horses lifted their heads, regarding them with calm, curious, dark eyes.

At last they came to a road paved with pieces of stone. "Our kin in the south learned how to do this from the Romans," Alfhjalm told him. "You can say what you want about the Romans, but they knew how to build roads."

Kormak barely knew who the Romans were. But he was glad to be walking on smooth pavement, rather than a twisting trail.

The road led to the long hall. When they were close, Kormak saw the roof was covered with shields. Some shone silver, others gold.

"They are bronze, covered with gold or silver leaf," Alfhjalm said. "It would be difficult to make the roof solid gold. We elves are more prosperous than Icelanders and have more precious metal, but our wealth is not unending. And if needed, we can pull the shields down and use them in war."

They entered the long hall. A fire burned low in a pit that ran the hall's length. At the end were two high seats made of carved wood. One was empty. The other contained a handsome old man. Firelight flickered over him, making his white hair and beard shine. He wore a crown, a simple band of gold, and a gold-hilted sword lay across his knees.

"This is Alfrad," Alfhjalm said. "Our lord."

They walked the length of the hall and bowed to the old man.

"Welcome," he said in a deep, impressive voice. "Tell me why you came here."

Kormak told the story of his journey with Egil and Svart and how the old man had killed Svart and tried to kill him, all to hide two chests of silver that he didn't want his son to inherit.

"They are a difficult family," the elf lord said finally. "Not good neighbors. I will send men to recover the silver in the river. There is no reason to leave it in the water. You will be our guest, until I decide what to do with you."

They bowed again and left the long hall. Once outside, Kormak gave a sigh of relief. He was not used to speaking with lords, especially elf lords. Alfhjalm took him to another building, where food lay on a table: bread and meat and ale. Kormak learned later that this happened often in Elfland. If something was needed — a meal, a tool, an article of clothing — it would be found close by, though he never saw servants bringing whatever it was. Maybe this was magic, or maybe the elves had servants who could not be seen: the Hidden Folk's hidden folk.

They sat down and ate. Kormak found he was hungry. "There are two high seats," he said to Alfhjalm, after he was full.

"The other belongs to Alfrad's wife Bevin. She is an Irish fey, who grew weary of the north and went home to Ireland, though she left a daughter here, who is named Svanhild. She is the loveliest maiden in Elfland and also the richest. I am courting her, along with many other men, but she is not interested in any of us."

"What is your quarrel with the family at Borg?" Kormak asked next. He was always curious. It was one of the qualities that made him a difficult slave.

"Manyfold," Alfhjalm replied. "We came to Iceland before humans did, leaving Norway because it became too crowded with people. There was no one here in those days, except a few Irish monks. We frightened them, and they kept to small islands off the coast, while we had all of Iceland for our own. The country was empty, except for birds and foxes. There were forests of birch and aspen, which the humans have cut down, and broad fields where we could pasture our animals, black mountains with caps of white snow, and the brilliant sky of summer. As lovely as Norway had been, this seemed lovelier.

"But then the settlers came. They were violent, greedy folk. We are less numerous than the elves of Norway, and we did not have the strength to oppose the settlers. We withdrew into the mountains to avoid them, becoming the Hidden Folk. When we traveled, it was at night, when no one could see us. That was our first quarrel with the Marsh Men. Egil's grandfather

Kveldulf would get sleepy late in the day and sit hunched in a corner of their hall. Then his spirit would go out in the form of a huge wolf, roaming through Borgarfjord. There are no wolves in Iceland, as you must know, only foxes and a few white bears that float into the northern fjords on sheets of ice."

Of course Kormak knew this. He had even seen the skin of a white bear, when he was a slave in the north. It had been yellow rather than white and not nearly as soft as a fox's pelt.

"The foxes are too small to bother us, and we don't have a problem with bears in this part of Iceland. But it was an ugly surprise when Kveldulf appeared in wolf form, and it made our night journeys unpleasant. He was a frightening sight in his wolf form. We elves do not like to be afraid."

No one did, thought Kormak.

"We thought of killing his wolf form, but it was possible that Kveldulf would be unharmed and wake up, knowing about us. Life was easier when we had Iceland — and Borgarfjord — to ourselves." Alfhjalm lifted a pitcher and poured more ale. "He died of old age finally, and the wolf was not seen again. Then his son Skallagrim inherited the farm at Borg. He was another man like Egil, big and strong and ugly, almost a giant; and he was an ironsmith, which sounds better than a wolf. But we elves are not entirely comfortable with iron, though we can use it and even work it. We prefer other metals. We are able to cast spells over copper, tin, silver, and gold, making the metal stronger, sharper, brighter, luckier, and better to use. Iron resists our magic. If we make an iron blade, it cuts less well than a blade of bronze. If we make an iron pot, it cooks food badly. Iron tools turn in our hands. Everything becomes less useful and lucky.

"Skallagrim made us uneasy, since he had great skill with iron, and we suspected his skill was magical. He never did us any harm. Nonetheless we avoided him and watched him for signs of danger. In the end, he died in bed like his father; and Egil became the farmer at Borg. He is the worst of the three: a Viking, a poet, and a magician. There is no question about his magical power, though it seems diminished now.

"He knows a spell that can compel land spirits, such as we are. He cast it on our kin in Norway, so they could not rest until they drove King Eirik Bloodaxe from the country. If he could do this to Norwegian elves, he can do it to us. It's a difficult spell that requires killing a mare and cutting off its head, then setting the head on a pole carved with runes. We are not sure he can still do it. But we are always careful around him."

"Why did you help me?" Kormak asked.

"I wanted to know what Egil was doing. He was killing men on our doorstep. Who could say what that meant? And he had a mare with him. It was possible that he planned to do magic.

"I am willing to cross him, if I can do it without him knowing. We have lived in fear of the Marsh Men for a long time, and it's been angering. Now it seems to be ending. Egil will die soon. Thorstein is a good farmer, but not at all magical. He will cause us no more trouble than any other human."

"What will happen to me?" Kormak asked.

"I think Alfrad will make you a slave. Do you have any special abilities?"

"I have worked with horses," Kormak said. He did not add that he'd learned some iron smithing from Svart.

"We have fine horses, as you have seen, and we take good care of them. You have a useful skill."

This was his fate, Kormak thought, to go from owner to owner, a slave to farmers in Iceland, then a slave to Icelandic elves. It was a discouraging idea. At least he was alive, unlike Svart, and he was away from the horrible old man. If it was his fate to labor for the elves, he would not trust them. Svart had trusted the Marsh Men.

He slept in an outbuilding. The next day the elf lord announced that Kormak would be a slave and sent him to work with the elf horses. They were intelligent, well-mannered animals, and Kormak enjoyed them.

All the slaves in Elfland were human. The elves did not own one another. But when humans came into their land, they enslaved them. There is always dirty work to be done everywhere, in Midgard and Alfheim and Jotunheim and Asgard. Even magical beings had work they did not want to do, either with their hands or with magic. The slaves were a miserable group, badly dressed, dirty, and sullen.

Kormak was sure he remembered stories about humans who went into Elfland and had fine lives, sleeping with elf ladies, hunting with elf lords, till they woke and realized a hundred years had passed. Instead he mucked out stables and groomed horses. Well, life was never like stories. In time, he began to help an elf smith, who forged gear for horses out of bronze. The smith had some iron, which he never used. "An evil metal," he told Kormak. But he kept the ingots tucked in a corner of his smithy, and Kormak remembered where the iron was.

So the days passed. There was no winter in Elfland, though the sky grew dark when winter came to the land outside. Still, it was warm. He never had to follow animals through the snow. One period of darkness came and went, then another, then a third. He had been in Elfland three years. Egil must be dead by now. Should he try to escape? Was it possible?

Elves came to get horses and ride them inside or outside Elfland. Some were tall and handsome men. Others were beautiful women. One was the lord's daughter, Svanhild. Her favorite mount was a dun mare with white mane and tail. No horse was lovelier, and no rider was more beautiful. Svanhild was blue-eyed with blond hair as white as her horse's mane. Her dress was usually blue, a deep and pure color. Her cloak was scarlet. Gold bracelets shone on her arms. Of course, Kormak was interested, but he was not crazy. He kept his ideas to himself and helped the elf girl on and off her horse.

One day she came by herself. The elf smith was gone from the forge, and Kormak worked alone. "I know you have been watching me," she said. "I think you want to have sex with me. I also know you are Irish, like my mother."

"I am Irish," said Kormak. "I am also a slave, and I take my pleasure with other slaves, not with noble women."

"That may be," Svanhild replied. "I want to go to my mother's country. My father is narrow-minded and avaricious. Look at what he did with the treasure you and your companion brought to the river. You don't have it. My father does, and he has not shared. Instead you are a slave, though you brought him wealth."

"Yes," said Kormak.

"The men here want to marry me, because I am my father's heir. I have no interest in any of them. In my mother's country, I might be free."

"Or maybe not," Kormak replied. "I have not found freedom anywhere."

"I am willing to try," Svanhild replied. "Will you come with me and help me?"

"Why should I?"

"Once we reach the land of the fey, I will set you free. You will be in Ireland then, which is your native country."

He would be taking a risk, but maybe it was time to do so. He did not want to spend the rest of his life as a slave in Elfland. Kormak answered, "Yes."

The woman smiled, and her smile was an arrow going into Kormak's heart.

She left, and he had a thought. While the elf smith was gone, he shod two horses with iron. One was Svanhild's favorite horse, the dun mare with white mane and tail. The other was an iron gray gelding with black mane and tail. The iron shoes made the horses uneasy. They sidled and danced. But they endured the iron.

Three days later, Svanhild returned. She rode a red mare and wore a chain mail shirt. Two full bags were fastened to her saddle.

"Is this the animal you want to take?" Kormak asked, disturbed. He was relying on the iron shoes.

"No. I needed it to carry my bags. But my dun mare is sturdier and better tempered."

Kormak unsaddled the animal and moved the saddle to the dun mare. As he did so, he noticed that the saddlebags were heavy. "I hope you have directions."

"I have a map, which my mother left me."

"Good." Kormak's horse was the gelding shod with iron. It was a strong horse, intelligent and calm. He did not want trouble on this journey. Fire was fine for war and stallion fights. But what he needed now was sturdy endurance.

They mounted. Svanhild led, and Kormak followed. This was hardly wise, he thought. He was risking his life for a girl who had no interest in him and for the hope of freedom. But he was tired of Elfland and Iceland.

They rode up a slope in the brief, dim daylight of winter, then entered a tunnel. The horses' hooves rang on stone. The air smelled of dust. There were only a few of the sun stone lamps here, possibly because the tunnel led down. Who would want to go away from sunlight and open air? A tunnel like this one must be little traveled.

Each lamp shone like a star in the distance. When they reached it, they traveled through a brief region of brightness, then back into darkness, with the next lamp shining dimly in front of them.

On and on they rode, till they reached a place with no more lamps. Svanhild reined her horse and opened a saddlebag. Out came a lamp made of bronze and glass. It was full of brightly shining sun stones. She gave it to Kormak to hold, then took out a bronze stick and unfolded it, till it became a long pole with a hook at one end. "Put the lamp on the hook," she told Kormak. "Then hold it up, so it casts light over us."

Kormak did as he was told.

They went on, riding slowly, lit by the lamp that Kormak held up.

At length they came to a spring that spurted out of the tunnel wall and flowed across the stone until it reached another hole and vanished. They dismounted and watered the horses, then drank themselves.

"How long is the journey?" Kormak asked.

"Twenty-five days by horse," the girl replied.

"Is it all like this?" Kormak asked, waving around at the tunnel.

"I think so."

"The horses will need to eat, and so will we."

"There are folk down here, dark elves mostly. They are kin to us, though they like darkness rather than light. We used to live in the sunlight, as I think you know. But they have always lived underground. This is their tunnel."

"Do they have hay?" Kormak asked.

"I think so."

They mounted and rode on.

There was no way to tell time in the darkness. But they continued until Kormak and the horses were tired. He was about to say they would have to stop, when a light appeared ahead of them. It wasn't a sun stone lamp, he realized as they came nearer. The light was too yellow and uncertain. It came from a lantern fixed to the tunnel's stone wall. A man stood under it, leaning on a spear. The still air smelled of hot oil.

He was as tall as one of the elf warriors, but broader through the shoulders and chest. His hair and beard were black. His skin was dark, and his eyes — glinting below heavy brows — were like two pieces of obsidian. He wore a mail shirt that shone like silver and a helmet inlaid with gold.

"What do we have here?" he asked in a deep voice.

"I am Svanhild, the daughter of Alfrad, a lord of the light elves and kin to you. This human is my slave. We are going to my mother's country in Ireland. I ask your help in getting there."

"I can't make that decision, as you ought to know. But I'll send you to those who can decide." He put two fingers in his mouth and whistled sharply. A dog emerged from the darkness, iron gray and wolfish. When it reached the elf warrior, it stopped. Its back was level with the warrior's belt, and every part of the animal was thick and powerful. A man could ride it, Kormak thought, if he pulled his feet up and the dog was willing.

It opened its mouth, revealing knife-sharp gray teeth and a gray tongue that lolled out.

It was iron, Kormak realized, though it moved as easily as a real dog. The dog regarded Kormak and the girl with eyes that glowed like two red coals.

"A marvel, isn't he?" the dark elf said. "Made of iron and magic. We can't do this kind of work any longer, but our ancestor Volund could. He made the dog after he fled the court of King Nidhad of Nerike, where he had been a prisoner. He took his revenge on Nidhad by killing the king's two sons and making goblets of their skulls and a broach of their teeth. He gave the goblets to the king and the broach to the king's wife, who was the boys' mother. In addition, because he was someone who did nothing by halves, he raped Bodvild, the king's lovely and innocent daughter. Then he flew away on iron wings. He couldn't walk, because the king had cut his hamstrings, wanting to keep Volund as a smith.

"Once he was safe, he forged the dog, working on crutches. He wanted a servant who was intelligent and trusty, but not any kind of man. By then he was tired of men, even of himself."

"What happened to the girl?" Svanhild asked.

"She had borne two children, products of the rape, which happened while she was in a drunken sleep, so she didn't know it had happened until she began to grow in size. Her father kept the boy, but put the girl out on a hillside to die. The child lived, but that's a story too long for me to tell." The dark elf looked down at the iron dog. "Take them to the Thing for All Trades."

The dog replied with a bark.

"Follow him," the dark elf ordered.

They did, riding into a side tunnel, dimly lit by a few oil lamps.

"What do you know about these people?" Kormak asked.

"They are ironsmiths, who use no magic. They say iron is sufficient and better than any other metal, though we think it's obdurate and uncooperative. I had not realized that Volund could enchant iron. He was a prince of the dark elves and famous for his skill as a smith.

"These days the dark elves have no princes, nor any lords. No one could equal Volund, they say. Instead, they form assemblies, where every elf has an equal voice."

"Like the Althing in Iceland," Kormak said. "Though rich and powerful men have more say there, and slaves have no say."

After a pause Svanhild said, "The dark elves do not distinguish between rich and poor or between men and women. All work, and all join the assembly for their trade."

"Why are they so different from you?" Kormak asked.

"Iron," Svanhild replied. "And lack of magic! All beauty and nobility comes from magic."

Kormak was not sure of this. There was little magic in Iceland, except for a few witches and men like Egil. But the black mountains and green fields seemed lovely to him, also the rushing rivers and the waves that beat against the country's coast. He could praise the flight of a falcon across the summer sky or the smooth gait of a running horse. At times he was at the edge of speaking poetry. But the words did not come; he was left with what he'd seen.

The tunnel opened into a cave. No sun stones shone from the cave's roof. Instead the floor was dotted with lights. Some looked to be lamps or torches. Others — brighter — might be forge fires. Hammers rang out, louder and more regular than any he'd heard before.

The dog kept going. They followed it down a slope. There was a track, lit by the lantern Kormak held: two ruts in the stony ground. It led into a little town. The low houses were built of stone. Lantern light shone from open doors and windows. Torches flared, fastened to exterior walls. Here and there, Kormak saw people: tall and powerful and dark. A woman swept her doorway. A man drove a pick, pulling cobbles out of the street.

Now they rode next to a stream, rushing between stone banks. Rapids threw up mist that floated in the air. Kormak felt it gratefully.

Ahead of them was a hall, torches blazing along its front. The stream ran before the hall, and a stone bridge crossed it. Two elven warriors stood on the bridge, armed with swords and metal shields.

Kormak and Svanhild reined their horses. "We were sent here by the guard in the tunnel," Svanhild said in her clear, pure voice. "I am Svanhild, the daughter of Alfrad, your kinswoman from the north."

"We know Alfgeir sent you, because the dog Elding is with you," one of the guards replied. "What do you want?"

"Passage to my mother's country in the south."

"Who is your mother?"

"Bevin of the White Arms."

"Irish fey," said the second guard. "We know them, though we don't much like them. Still, it's up to the thing-chiefs to decide your fate." He turned and pushed through the hall's metal door.

They waited for a while, staying on their horses. Finally, the guard came back out. "Go in."

Svanhild and Kormak dismounted.

The first guard said, "I'll water your horses while you're gone. They are fine animals, better than any we have, though they look weary and thirsty."

"Not too much water," Kormak warned.

"We know iron better than animals. Nonetheless, we have some horses, and I have cared for them. I know what to do."

They walked inside, the iron dog pacing next to them. The hall was as large as Alfrad's. Stone pillars held up the roof, and stone benches ran along the two sidewalls, unoccupied at present. A long fire pit ran down the middle, full of ash. Here and there red light shone from the ash, and a thin trail of smoke rose. But most of the light came from torches burning around the high seats at the hall's far end. There were six. Three held old men with broad, white beards; and three held old women with long, white braids. The dog barked. Kormak and Svanhild walked forward and bowed to the thing-chiefs.

"Who are you?" an old woman asked, leaning forward. She was bone thin, with a skin the gray hue of a twilight sky. Her eyes were dark and keen.

"Svanhild, the daughter of Alfrad. My father is an elf lord and your kin, as he has often told me. This man is my slave."

He was tired of this introduction, Kormak thought, but said nothing.

"Why have you come?" an old man asked. He was darker than the woman, though his skin had the same faint tint of blue. His eyes were as pale as ice.

"I seek help in reaching my mother's country in Ireland."

"Why should we help?" another woman asked, this one fat and black. She had blue eyes that looked like stars to Kormak. No woman this old should have eyes so bright.

The dog opened its mouth and spoke in a harsh voice that Kormak could barely understand.

> "Hat-hidden, Odin
> tests human hosting.
> Hard the fate
> of those who fail."

"Nonsense," another old man, as gray as granite, put in. "We are not human, and both of these people have two eyes."

"And no ravens," the third old man said. He was the palest of the chiefs. "They are not Odin."

The third woman, twilight colored like the first woman, said, "The All-Father judges all, not just humans; and the dog reminds us that he requires hospitality."

The black woman leaned forward. "But in honor of our ancestor Volund, we need to ask for fair payment for what we do — in gold or silver, stories, music, or revenge."

"I can pay," Svanhild replied. "We came here with two horses. One is a gelding, but the other is a fine mare, able to improve your breed. I will give the horses to you in return for our passage."

"That seems fair," the black woman said. "Two good horses for a ride in one of our lightning carts. They will be going to Ireland and Wales, even if there are no passengers."

"Why?" asked Kormak, the man who asked questions.

"Why do they go?" the palest man answered, stroking his silky beard. "They go to Ireland to deliver jewels and fine smithing to the fey there. No iron, of course. The fey hate iron. They go to Wales for coal. We mine it from below and send it to our forges in the north."

"Are you willing to give us passage?" Svanhild asked.

One by one, the elf chiefs nodded.

"Come with me," a voice said next to Kormak. It was Alfgeir, the guard in the tunnel. He must have followed them, Kormak thought, and slipped into the hall while they waited outside. He wore a cloak now, as if he planned to travel. "I know the woman's name. But who are you?"

Kormak introduced himself as the elf warrior led them from the hall. The two guards were still there, watering the horses in the stream.

"These are ours now," Alfgeir said. "It was clever of you to shoe them with iron. Svanhild's kin could not track them with magic."

"I thought that might be true," said Kormak. "I did not know for certain."

Svanhild gestured at her mare, and Kormak took off the saddlebags, staggering a little under their weight. What had the elf maid packed? He lifted the bags over one shoulder and followed Alfgeir and Svanhild. She had the lantern. It lit their way to the edge of town.

A low platform stood there. Torches on poles cast a wavering light. They climbed onto the platform. Kormak walked to the far side and looked down, seeing ground covered with gravel. Planks of wood lay in the gravel. Two, long narrow pieces of iron lay across the wood. It looked like a fence lying down.

"Where do you get the wood?" he asked.

"From Ireland," said Alfgeir. "They have mighty forests of oak and pine and birch."

"What's it for?"

"You will see."

After a while Kormak heard a noise he didn't recognize. He looked toward it and saw a lantern coming out of the darkness. The noise grew louder. The light kept coming, growing larger and brighter. Kormak stepped away from the platform's edge.

The thing, whatever it was, lurched and rattled closer. He stepped farther back as the thing slowed and came to a stop. It was a metal cart with a tall metal tube rising from its roof. Smoke billowed from the tube. Fire burned within the cart, and two figures moved there, lit by the red glare. He couldn't make out what they were doing.

Behind the cart was a second cart, full of pieces of shiny, black rock. Beyond this were more carts, some with roofs and others open. The elf warrior pointed at one of the roofed carts. "Get in."

They did and found it contained metal benches, set along the walls like benches in a long hall. Kormak put the saddlebags down. The dog lay down next to them, its gray tongue hanging out between sharp, gray teeth. The three of them sat down on the metal benches. The cart jerked, and then the entire thing, whatever it was, moved forward. They left the platform behind and went into darkness, except for the dog's red eyes and the lantern that Svanhild held.

For a long time they rattled along. Either the cavern was huge, or they were going from one cave to another. Sometimes the region around them was completely dark. Sometimes there were clusters of lights, more stone towns maybe, or great, flaring forges with gigantic hammers that rose and fell. The hammers were far too large to be held by men or elves. Nonetheless, they moved. Kormak saw no sign of trolls.

Svanhild's lantern cast enough light so he could see both of his companions. The elf warrior sprawled on a bench, looking comfortable. Svanhild sat stiffly, her face expressionless. Afraid, thought Kormak, as was he. The iron dog panted gently.

At last, the line of carts slowed and stopped.

"This can't be Ireland," Svanhild said, looking around at the darkness.

Alfgeir laughed. "We are a long distance from your mother's country. But we are about to enter the tunnel that goes under the ocean. We can't use fire devices there. Out here, in the caves, the smoke rises and spreads out. But the tunnel is low and narrow. Smoke would fill it, and we'd choke. Workers used to die in the tunnel, before we invented the lightning devices."

There were noises outside their cart, movement and some light, but Kormak could not see enough to understand what was happening.

"We are changing devices," the elf warrior said. "Before, our power came from burning coal. Now it will come from a fluid that we call lightning, since it shares qualities with Thor's lightning, though it is quieter and better behaved. Our smiths have taught it to run in copper wires. We fasten these to the roof of the tunnel. A rod brings the fluid into our new device, and it moves without fire or smoke."

"Another wonder," Svanhild said in a calm tone.

Alfgeir said, "Much can be achieved without magic. We do not trick or compel materials against their nature. Instead, we learn what each material can do."

The activity outside stopped, and the carts moved forward again. The smoke that had whirled around them was gone, and there was less noise, though the carts still clanked and rattled.

"The lands of the elves are full of wonders," Svanhild said. "But they do not equal my mother's country."

"Wait and see," Alfgeir said.

"How can you raise horses in this darkness?" Kormak asked.

"We pasture them outside in high valleys or on unsettled

islands. It's been harder since humans settled Iceland and Greenland. In the end, we may give the pastures up and keep our livestock in caves lit by lightning. The animals are likely to do less well without sunlight, and so we hesitate."

"Why don't you use sun stones?" Svanhild asked.

"Surely you realize they are magic. They would fade quickly here. We use too much iron."

Kormak looked at the lantern Svanhild held. Yes. It was dimmer than before.

"This journey is boring," Svanhild said.

"Then I will entertain you by telling you more of the story of Volund, our ancestor," Alfgeir said.

"Very well," said Svanhild.

"King Nidhad went to Volund's forge and said, 'Where are my children?'

"'I will tell you,' Volund replied. 'But first you must make me a promise. If a child of mine ever enters your court, you must do no harm to him.'

"This seemed like a simple request. Odin encourages us to be hospitable, as you have found out; and as far as Nidhad knew, Volund had no children.

"So he promised. Of course he was a fool. Volund told him that the two boys were dead. Their skulls were the king's gold and ivory drinking cups. Their teeth were the queen's gold and ivory broach.

"Nidhad drew his sword, intending to slay Volund, but not yet. 'What about Bodvild, my lovely and innocent daughter?'

"'She lies drunk. She came to my forge, looking for fine jewelry. Instead, I gave her ale and raped her when she was not able to resist.'

"Nidhad raised his sword. In reply, Volund raised his arms, on which were magical iron wings. Before the king could reach him, he brought the wings down, lifting himself into the air.

'Remember your promise, king,' he called, and flew away.

"That was the last Nidhad saw of Volund. As for his daughter, she grew big and bigger and gave birth to twins: a boy and a girl. Nidhad considered his promise. He had said he would not harm a child, but here were two. Did his promise cover both? It seemed reasonable to keep the boy and put the girl on a hillside.

"The boy was named Vidga. Bodvild nursed him and raised him. His grandfather the king treated him harshly, remembering the two fine boys he had lost. Why should Volund have a son, when he had none? As soon as the boy was able, he left home. He became a famous hero, a soldier for the great king Thidrik of Bern. In the end he died, as heroes do.

"As for the girl, a farmwife found her crying on the hillside. She was a woman who had no children, and even a girl seemed worth saving. She gathered the baby up and carried her home, where she fed her with a piece of cloth soaked in milk. Sucking on this, the baby grew strong.

"She was raised to be a farmwife, though her father was an elf prince and her mother was the daughter of a king.

"The farmwife named the girl Alda, which means wave. She took after her mother as far as appearances went, being blond and fair skinned with eyes like blue stars. But she had her father's skill with materials, though — in her case — it came out as spinning and weaving. The thread she spun was like gossamer. The cloth she wove was like silk, though it was made of wool, taken from sturdy Swedish sheep.

"When she worked spinning or weaving, Alda sang:

> 'What is my fate?
> Where is my husband?
> Who will I be
> In ten years or more?'

"One day a fey, wandering far from his native soil, heard her song and followed the sound of her voice. It's rare to find fey in Scandinavia. For the most part, they keep to their Irish mounds. But this man, who was named Hogshead, came to Alda's house. There she sat, outside in the sunlight, spinning thread that shone like gold.

"Of course, the fey had to have her. Of course, she could not resist a handsome man, dressed in fine clothes and wearing gold rings on his wrists and fingers.

"Without a word to the people who had raised her, she left her spindle and the house. Together, they followed the hidden ways that go from Europe to the Atlantic islands. When they reached Ireland and entered the fey's home mound, he changed. His body remained as it had been, but his head turned into the head of a huge, hairy, ugly boar with jutting tusks and little, hard eyes.

"Alda was her father's daughter. She did not scream, as most human women would, and her expression did not change, but she took a step back.

"The fey made a grunting sound that might have been a laugh. Then he bowed deeply. As he straightened, his head changed, and he was once again a handsome man. 'You don't like my true appearance?'

"'No,' said Alda.

"'Well, then, I suppose we have no future. I like to be comfortable at home and look the way I am. Nonetheless, you must meet our queen.'

"He led her to the mound's queen, who was — and is — your mother, though this was long before she married Alfrad. Hogshead told the queen about Alda's spinning and weaving.

"'Show me,' the queen said.

"A spindle and loom were brought, along with wool. Alda spun the wool into yarn and wove it into a fine, thin cloth.

"'You must make my clothes!' the queen exclaimed. 'But not out of wool. We'll find you silk, and I'll be the envy of all the fey in Ireland!'

"There Alda remains in Ireland, in the mound. She has learned to spin and weave silk, and she makes the queen the finest clothing in Ireland."

"That's it?" Kormak asked.

"So far."

"That isn't much of an ending. She should have escaped from the fey or died. That's the way most stories end. A victory or death. Why didn't Volund rescue her?"

"We can't find him to ask him. Maybe the dog knows where he is."

The iron dog lifted its head but said nothing.

"He always cared more for his craft than for any person, except — possibly — his Valkyrie wife, who left him. It's said that he always frowned deeply and grew grim when he heard 'yo-to-ho.'"

After that, Kormak grew sleepy and lay down, waking now and then to the rattle of the cart over its metal trail. The lantern had grown dimmer, and the cart was mostly dark. Sometimes he saw the red glare of the dog's eyes.

At length, he woke completely and sat up. Svanhild and the elf warrior sat together near the lantern, sharing bread and wine in its glow. Kormak joined them. There were mushrooms in addition to bread. Alfgeir laid these between two pieces of bread and ate the result. Kormak followed suit. The mushrooms were delicious, thick and meaty and juicy. The bread was a little dry. He drank enough wine to feel it, then sat by a window and looked out. The lantern on the foremost cart lit the tunnel's stone walls and the metal track ahead of it. Now and then, a second light flashed above the cart, brilliant and white.

"That is the lightning," Alfgeir said.

So it went. Kormak dozed and slept. They ate a second time. The sun stone lantern had gotten dimmer.

"Tell me about my mother's land," Svanhild said.

"Didn't she tell you about it?" the elf warrior asked.

"Only that it was far more pleasant than my father's country. She left when I was young."

"We live in stone," Alfgeir said. "As do you. But the fey live below earthen mounds. Their underground country does not look like a cave, as do our homes, but rather like open land, though the sky is sunless and moonless. Magic lights it. There is no winter. The trees bear flowers and fruit at the same time. The streams are full of cold, fresh water. The ground is covered with soft, green grass like a carpet.

"When the fey hunt — and they do; it's their favorite occupation — they bring down fat deer. When they angle, they bring up succulent fish. Everything about their land is lovely and rich.

"They love music and dancing and good-looking people like Volund's daughter Alda. They keep them as servants and lovers."

They would not love him, Kormak thought, with the scar across his face. Well, he had no desire to live among the fey. He remembered them dimly from stories he'd heard as a child. They were more dangerous than the northern elves, who mostly kept to themselves and did not bother their neighbors.

The iron dog growled and spoke:

> "Brightness is not best.
> Honor is better.
> Loveliness leads nowhere
> If the heart is hard."

"That may be," Alfgeir said. "But you do not know for certain, Elding. You have never been in their country, nor spent time with any of them." He looked to Kormak and Svanhild. "When we get close to the land of the fey, the carts will stop, and you will have to walk. The fey do not tolerate iron in their country. The dog cannot come. Nor can I. I will not give up my iron."

Kormak went back to sleep and woke again. The sun stone lantern was so dim that his companions were barely visible, though he could still find the dog by the glare of its eyes.

They finished off the rest of the food and wine in silence. Then Kormak sat in darkness, listening to the cart rattle on and on. There was nothing else to do. He slept again and woke and found the carts were motionless. A pale light, like the dawn through mist, shone outside. He could see a platform and a tunnel leading up.

Svanhild lay on the bench opposite him, sleeping and snoring softly, like a cat purring.

"We are here," Alfgeir said. "She won't wake soon, so we have time to talk."

"How do you know she won't wake?" Kormak asked.

"She drank the rest of the wine. That by itself should have put her deeply asleep, but I added a spell."

"You said that dark elves do no magic."

Alfgeir grinned, showing square, white teeth. "No elf is entirely trustworthy, though we are far more reliable than the fey. For the most part, I have told you the truth. Iron makes magic difficult, and dark elves rarely perform it. We always prefer iron. But we're a long way from our country here and close to the country of the fey. Magic is easier here. I have something I want you to do."

"What?" asked Kormak.

"Go into the country of the fey with Svanhild."

"Why should I do this?"

"Look around you. There is nothing here except stone, and it's a long walk back to the country of the dark elves. Dangerous, too. You might be hit by one of our trains. You could go the other direction, of course, and end up in the coal mines of Wales. If you do as I ask, I will be grateful."

"What is your gratitude worth to me?"

"Enough silver to establish yourself among the humans of Ireland. You will be free, and you will be an elf friend."

"That sounds good," Kormak said. "What do you want me to do?"

Alfgeir pulled a bag from somewhere in his clothing and took a gold bracelet out. "Look for Alda in the fey court. Get her alone and give her this. Tell her to wear it on her arm, but keep it hidden under her sleeve. If the fey see it, they will steal it from her."

"Yes," Kormak said, and took the bracelet.

"The second time you see her, give her this." Alfgeir pulled out a gold and ivory broach. "Tell her to pin it to her undergarment, so it will be hidden from the fey. Make sure that she knows to pin it over her heart."

"Do you think she will do this?" Kormak asked.

"She is the child of her mother and the grandchild of Nidhad's queen. Both women loved gold." The elf warrior took a final object from his bag. It was a golden dog, small enough to be held in a woman's hand. The eyes were garnets. A golden tongue hung out between tiny, sharp ivory teeth.

"The third time, you won't have to seek her out. She will come to you. Give her this, and see what happens."

"Very well," Kormak said. He put the three objects in their bag and hid the bag in his clothing.

"Now," said Alfgeir. He touched the sleeping woman, and she woke. "Go into the tunnel. It will lead you to the country of the fey."

Svanhild climbed out of the iron cart. Kormak followed, carrying Svanhild's bags, which had not become any easier to carry. They walked along the platform and into the tunnel. Light filled it. There was no point of origin; the air itself seemed to glow, and he could only see a short distance. The glowing whiteness closed in like a mist. The tunnel slanted up and twisted like a snake, rising and turning. They began to climb.

This went on for a long time, till he was weary from carrying Svanhild's saddlebags. If the dark elf had been telling the truth, he would come out of this with freedom and silver. That was worth some effort. Did he trust the elf? Not entirely. But what choice did he have? He had learned one thing when the northerners came to his village and burned it and took slaves. He did not control his fate.

At last they came to a door made of polished wood and covered with carvings of interlaced animals. Set in the door was a bronze ring. Svanhild took hold and knocked.

The door opened, revealing a handsome man in green. His hair was red and curly. His face was clean shaven, and his skin was fair. He wore a heavy, twisted, golden torque around his neck. "Well?" he asked.

"I am Svanhild, the daughter of Bevin of the White Arms. I've come to find my mother."

"She's here, though I don't know if she will want to see you. Nonetheless, come in."

They did. As Kormak passed through the doorway, the stone groaned loudly. The man looked suddenly wary. "What are you?"

"He's human and my slave," Svanhild said. "Don't you have human slaves?"

"Why should we? We are served by magical beings. Humans are for making music and love. Since he belongs to you, I will let him in."

Beyond the door was a wide, green country. A meadow lay in front, where noble-looking people played a bowling game with golden balls. On the far side, the land rose into wooded hills. Many of the trees were flowering. A sweet scent filled the air. The sky above was misty white.

"I will escort you to the queen," the man said.

"Do you have a name?" Kormak asked.

"My name is Secret," the fey replied. "And you?"

"Kormak."

"Are you Irish?"

"Yes."

"Our favorite humans!"

They circled the meadow to avoid the bowlers. A wood bridge led over a crystal-clear river. Looking down, Kormak saw silver trout floating above the river's pebbled floor. Apple trees with fragrant white blossoms leaned over the water, dropping petals. He saw red fruit among the blooms. A miraculous land!

The next thing he knew they were climbing a hill. On top was a grove of oak trees, their branches thick with acorns. The ground was carpeted with acorns, and a huge boar was feeding. Its lean body was covered with long, black, bristling hair, and yellow tusks sprouted from its mouth.

Svanhild paused. "Is this safe?"

"That's Hogshead," the fey answered. "He'll do us no harm."

The boar lifted its head, then reared up till it was standing on its hind legs. Kormak had never seen any kind of pig do this. A moment later, a man dressed in scarlet stood where the boar had been.

"How are the acorns?" their fey asked.

The man grunted happily, and they walked on, leaving him standing under the oak trees.

Well, that was strange, Kormak thought. He glanced at Svanhild. Usually she had a calm, determined expression. But now she looked drunk or dazed, her eyes wide open and her lips parted. Was this Alfgeir's magic? Or was she so in love with her mother's land?

They descended the hill to another meadow. A silver tent stood in the middle. The fabric shone like water and moved like water in the gentle wind.

"This is her bower," their fey said.

One side was open. Inside sat richly dressed ladies, listening to a harper play. Some had human heads and faces. Others had the heads of deer with large ears and large, dark eyes. One had the long neck and sharp, narrow beak of a heron, though her shoulders — white and sloping — were those of a woman, and she had a woman's graceful arms and hands.

In the middle sat the queen, who looked human, more fair than any woman Kormak had ever seen. She held up a hand to silence the harper, then beckoned.

They approached. "Who are you?" the queen asked.

"I am Svanhild, the daughter of Alfrad and Bevin of the White Arms. This man is human and a slave."

"If that is so, you are my daughter. If you wish, you can stay awhile. But the human is ugly, scarred, and worn with labor. Send him away. Maybe someone in my land will find him interesting. But I don't want to look at him."

Svanhild glanced at Kormak. "Do as the queen says. Put down my saddlebags and go."

Kormak did as he was told. The harper began playing. The music was sweeter than any he had heard before, and he would have liked to stay. But the queen had a cold face. What had the iron dog called it? Beauty with a hard heart.

Their fey walked with him from the tent.

"What will I do?" Kormak asked.

"There are humans here who no longer interest us. Former lovers. Former harpers and pipers. They live in our forests.

When we have finished banquets — we usually eat out of doors, so we can enjoy the scented air and the birds that fly from tree to tree — they come and eat whatever food remains. Sometimes we hunt them for amusement."

This was worse than living in Elfland. It might even be worse than Iceland.

"Do you know a banquet that might be over?" Kormak asked. "I'm hungry."

The fey pointed. Kormak walked through the lush, green grass to a grove of apple trees. He pulled an apple from among the blossoms and ate as he walked. In the middle of the grove was a long table made of wooden boards. Dishes covered it, full of the remains of a feast: roast pork, white bread, wine, a half-eaten salmon. Ragged humans fed there, using their hands. He joined in. Everything was delicious, though cold.

"Do you know the human woman Alda?" he asked when he was full.

The man next to him stopped chewing on a ham bone and said, "There's a cave in that far hill." He used the ham bone to point. "She's there, always weaving. She won't pay any attention to you. She's under an enchantment, as I used to be, when the noble lady Weasel loved me. I wish I still were. I was happy then. Now I am not."

Kormak went on. Maybe he should have refused this task. But that would have left him in the stone tunnel, with no alternative except to walk back to the land of dark elves.

A trail, no more than an animal track, wound through forest and meadow. He followed it to the hill. As the man had said, there was a cave. Lamps shone inside. Kormak entered. A woman sat at a loom, weaving. She was young with long, blond hair. For a human, she was lovely, though not as lovely as the fey with human heads.

He greeted her. She kept weaving, paying him no attention.

What could he do? He took out the gold bracelet and held it between her and the loom. She paused. "What is this?"

"A gift for you. Take it and wear it. But be sure to keep it under your sleeve. The fey will steal it if they see it."

"This is true." She took the bracelet and pushed it onto her arm, under the sleeve. Then she looked at Kormak. Her blue eyes were dim, as if hidden by a fine veil. "Who are you?"

"An emissary from someone who wants to give you gifts. I know no more than that."

"Is there more?" the woman asked.

"Yes, but not today."

"I could tell the fey about you."

"And lose the gifts. You know the fey share little."

The woman nodded. "I have been here a long time, weaving and weaving. They have never given me gold, though they have plenty." Then she went back to weaving.

Kormak left her and went up into the forest on the hill. He found a clearing in a pine grove, where the air was sweet with the scent of pine. One huge tree had a hollow at its base. He used that as a bed.

In the middle of the night, he woke. A splendid stag stood in front of him, rimmed with light.

"What are you?" Kormak asked.

"I used to be human. Now I am prey. Can you hide me?"

Kormak scrambled up and looked at his hollow, then at the stag. "You are too big."

"I will have to run," the stag replied and ran.

As it left his little clearing, dogs appeared, baying loudly. After them came fey on horseback with bows and spears. Kormak crouched down. They did not seem to see him. Instead they raced through the clearing and were gone.

The stag had no chance. The light that rimmed him made him a clear target. He would die. Kormak wrapped his arms around his knees and shook. Finally he went back to sleep. In the morning, he remembered the stag dimly. Had it been a dream?

The day was misty, as if the silver-white sky had descended and hung now among the hilltops. Trees were shadowy. The air felt damp. Kormak wandered down into meadows, looking for another banquet. He found nothing. In the end, he picked apples from among the apple blossoms and ate them to break his fast. In spite of the mist, the land looked more beautiful than on the previous day. Flowers shone like jewels in the grass. The birds sang more sweetly than any birds he'd ever heard, even as a child in Ireland. The birds in Iceland had not been singers. Instead they had quacked, honked, whistled, and screamed.

He reached Alda's cave and entered. She sat at her loom, her hands unmoving. "I dreamed of my foster parents last night and the farm where I grew up. How could I have forgotten?"

"I know nothing about that," Kormak replied. "But here is your second gift." He held out the gold and ivory broach. "Pin it to your undergarment, over your heart, and make sure the fey do not see it."

Alda did as he said. "I feel restless today, unwilling to weave."

"Do you have to?"

"The queen will be angry if I don't."

"Does she come here often?"

"No."

He sat down, leaning against the cave wall, and they talked. He told her about his life in Iceland and among the light elves, though he didn't tell her about Alfgeir or the dark elves.

She talked about her foster family. It was hard to talk about the fey, she said. Events in their country were hard to remember. "My dream last night is clearer to me than my days here."

At last, he rose. "I will come again."

"Yes," said Alda.

He walked out. The mist had lifted, and the land lay bright under the white sky. Kormak's heart rose. He spent the rest of the day wandering. Deer grazed in meadows. A sow with piglets drank from a crystal stream. Once a cavalcade of fey rode by. He stepped into the shadow of trees and watched the fey, admiring their embroidered garments, gold torques, and gold crowns.

The white sky slowly darkened. At length he found the remains of a banquet. Torches on poles blazed around it, and ragged humans fed at the board. He joined them, gathering bread, roasted fowl, and wine.

He ate until a fey appeared. It was short and looked like a badger, covered with gray fur, with white stripes on its head. Unlike any animal Kormak had seen before, it wore pants and shoes. The pants were bright blue and the shoes red. The badger's beady eyes were intelligent, and it could speak. "Away! Away! You miserable vermin! Eat acorns in the forest! Eat worms in the meadows! Don't eat the food of your betters!"

Kormak ran. No one followed him. After wandering awhile, he found the hollow where he'd slept the night before. He settled down and slept. In the morning, he woke to a kind of daze. His promises to Alfgeir and Alda no longer seemed important. Why should he visit the weaver in the cave? Why should he deliver the golden dog? It seemed more reasonable to wander in the woods and meadows, watching the fey from a distance, admiring their beauty.

That day — or another — he found a well and leaned over the stone wall that rimmed it. Below was water. A salmon rose to the surface and said, "Well, you are a sad case."

"What do you mean?" Kormak asked, not surprised that the fish could talk.

"You were given a task, but you have not completed it. Instead, you have let the country of the fey enchant you."

"It's better than Iceland or Elfland," Kormak said.

"There is more than one kind of slavery," the salmon replied and dove.

He left the well, dismissing the salmon's words.

He had no idea how many days passed after that. The sky darkened and then grew light, but there was never sun or moon to keep time. He remembered meals, though not well, and tumbling in a pine needle bed with a woman, not a fey, but a ragged human. They were both drunk. After, she told him of the days when she had been the lover of a noble fey. Everything had been magical then: the fey's loving, the wine, the gowns she wore, the music and dancing.

The woman left in the morning. He had a terrible hangover and slept most of the day. More time passed. He had more food, but no more sex. One morning he woke and saw Alda standing by his hollow. "You didn't come back," she said.

"I forgot," he said after a moment.

"That can happen here. It's dangerous. Always try to remember. You said you had one more gift for me."

He dug in the earth of his sleeping hollow till he found the bag Alfgeir had given him.

"I have dreamed of my childhood every night," Alda said. "My foster parents and our neighbors. Ordinary things, though sometimes — not often — I have dreamed of a man working in a forge, leaning on crutches, his legs withered. His shoulders are wide and strong, his hammer blows powerful. I don't know who he was."

Volund, thought Kormak. But how could she dream of a man she had never met?

Alda continued. "This country seems dim now. I no longer find it attractive, and weaving has become tiresome. I want to return to the land outside. I suspect you may know the way. So I came to find you."

Kormak scrambled to his feet. He pulled out the gold dog with garnet eyes, the last of Alfgeir's gifts, and Alda took it. As soon as it was in her hand, the gold shell split in two. Inside was a dog made of black metal. Alda cried out and dropped the tiny thing. As soon as it was on the ground, it began to grow larger and larger, until it was the size of an Icelandic horse.

"Mount me," it growled. "I will carry you from this place."

"Will you do this?" Kormak asked Alda.

"Yes."

"You as well, Kormak," the dog growled.

He hesitated.

"The fey will punish you, when they find Alda gone," the dog growled.

They mounted the iron dog, Kormak first, Alda behind him, her arms around his waist.

The moment they were on the dog, the sky darkened.

"The fey know I'm here," the dog said. "Though there is little they can do, except send apparitions. Their magic cannot harm me, nor you as long as you ride me. Hold tight! And ignore what you see!"

Frozen rain began to fall, hitting them like stones. The dog ran. Monsters emerged from the gray sleet: animals like wolves, but much larger. They paced the dog, snarling and snapping. Then the ground, covered with hail, began to move. Other monsters rose from it, long and sinuous and white. Kormak had no idea what they were. Their mouths were full of sharp teeth, and liquid dripped from their narrow tongues. Was it poison? The dog kept running, leaping from monster to monster, never slipping on the wet, scaly backs. Like the wolves, the worms snapped. But they could not reach the dog or its riders.

The storm ended suddenly. They ran among flowering trees.

Lovely men and women paced them now, riding on handsome horses. "Don't leave, dear Alda. Whatever you want, we'll give you."

Alda's arms tightened around Kormak's waist.

"And you, Kormak? What do you want? Gold? A fey lover? Music, rare food, dancing? In the land outside, you will be a slave again. Here you can be a noble lord."

The air around them filled with harping. Dancers appeared among the flowering trees.

"Run faster," Alda cried.

The dog entered a tunnel. Flying things pursued them: giant dragonflies and little birds with teeth. They darted around the dog, almost touching. The wings of the dragonflies whirred loudly. The little birds cried, "Return! Return!"

"Don't bat at them," the dog barked. "If you touch them, you will lose the safety I give you!"

Holes appeared in the tunnel floor. The dog leaped these easily, undistracted by the birds and dragonflies. Looking down as the dog passed over, Kormak saw deep pits. Some held water, where huge fish swam. Others held fire.

The tunnel ended in a door. The dog paused and lifted a foreleg, striking the wood. It split.

They passed through and were outside, in the green land of Ireland. Hills rolled around them, covered with forest. The sun shone down. A man stood waiting.

It was Alfgeir, of course. He looked older and more formidable than he had before, and his legs were encased in iron rods, with hinges at the knees. The rods were inlaid with silver patterns that glinted in the Irish sunlight.

"Don't get off the dog, till you have heard what I have to say," he told them. "Kormak, you have been in the realm of the elves and fey for thirty years. When you step down and touch the ground, you will be more than fifty. Consider whether you want to do this. Alda, you have been among the fey for many centuries. You are part elf, and we age more slowly than humans. Still, you will be much older if you touch the ground."

"What alternative do we have?" Kormak asked.

"I can tell the dog to carry you into the country of the elves. You will remain your present ages there."

"I am tired of magic," Alda said. "I will risk age in order to live in sunlight." She slid down from the dog, standing on the green turf of Ireland. As soon as she did this, she changed, becoming an upright, handsome old woman with silver hair. Her blue eyes shone brightly, no longer veiled. Although her face was lined, it was still lovely.

"And you, Kormak?" Alfgeir asked.

He sat awhile on the iron dog, looking over the hills of Ireland. Thirty years! Well, he had experienced a lot in that time: the light elves, the dark elves, the fey. He could not say the time was wasted. Like Alda, he was tired of enchantments; and Alda — old though she might be — looked better to him than the fey or their human slaves. Lack of aging made the fey indolent and selfish, while their human slaves became greedy and envious. The Icelanders had been better. They knew about old age and death. The best of them — the heroes — faced it fighting, like Egil.

It surprised him that he thought of Egil with approval. The old monster! The killer! How angry he must have been at his son and his dying body! That was no excuse for killing Svart. He would do better, Kormak thought. He could not excel Egil in fighting, but he could excel him in growing old.

"I will risk age as well." He swung down off the dog. As he touched the ground, he felt his body thicken. He was heavier than before, though still strong. A gray beard bristled over his chest. He brushed his hand across it. Hairs prickled against his palm.

"Well, then," Alfgeir said. "I ought to tell you my true name. It's Volund. I am Alda's father. I could not enter the country of the fey to rescue her. The doors into the land of the fey have wards against anything that is foreign and might be dangerous: humans, iron, unfamiliar magic, and magicians who are not fey. My leg braces are iron and magic, and they cannot be made otherwise. In addition, I am a great magician. The fey doors would have roared like dragons if I had tried to enter.

"The fey let you in, because you seemed harmless.

"I gave you three magical gifts to give Alda. The first two would wake her and break the magical bonds that held her, because they contain what the fey hate most: death and history. As much as possible, they try to live beyond time and change. Memory fails in their country. Although they love to hunt, they do not like to touch blood or death. Their human slaves strike the killing blow and butcher the animals.

"But, as Odin said:

> 'Cattle die. Kinsman die.
> You yourself will die.
> I know one thing that does not die.
> The fame of the dead.'

"That is what's real for humans: blood and death and history; and that is what I gave to Alda with my first two gifts.

"Bodvild asked me to make the bracelet, when she came to my forge. Foolish child! Later, when she lay drunk on the smithy floor, I raped her, breaking her maidenhead, and took back the bracelet. She was your mother, Alda."

"A cruel gift," Alda said.

"The broach was made for your grandmother. The ivory in it is the teeth of your uncles. I killed them and made their skulls into drinking cups. Their teeth became a broach, which I recovered before I flew from Nidhad's court. I left the cups for Nidhad to enjoy."

Alda's hands went to her breast, touching the broach under her dress. "Another cruel gift."

"Yes," Volund said. "But remember the third gift. The dog could not enter the land of the fey, any more than I could. But hidden in its golden shell and carried by you, Kormak, it could slip in. When the shell broke, it could carry you away."

"Why did it take you so long?" asked Kormak, always curious. "Alda was a prisoner for centuries. Did you not care for her at all?"

"How could he?" Alda asked. "I come from blood and death."

Volund smiled, showing strong, square, white teeth. "I am comfortable with blood and death, as my history ought to tell you; and kin matter to me. I knew your brother, Alda, and made him a sword that he used until he died. A famous warrior! But not as lucky as he might have been.

"It took me a long time to learn that Alda was still alive and then find where she had gone. Then — hardest of all — I had to find someone who could enter the land of the fey unsuspected. You could, Kormak. A human and a slave. No one would fear you or suspect you, since you came with Svanhild."

"What will happen to her?" Kormak asked.

"She is as hard-hearted as her mother. You must have noticed that. She will be fine among the fey. Her father may try to recover her, but I doubt that she will go back.

"I promised you silver," Volund added. He bent down and lifted two bags. "This is the silver that Egil hid in the waterfall. Svanhild stole it from her father, so she would have a gift to give her mother. I took it from her while she was sleeping on the train. The treasure you carried into the land of the fey is gravel, enchanted to look like silver. When you entered, did the doorway groan?"

"Yes," said Kormak.

"That was because you are human, and also because you carried magic — the gravel and the three gifts. Since you were not turned away, the guard must have thought the door was groaning for only one reason."

"Yes."

Volund grinned again. "The spell on the gravel will wear off, but this is real. You are a rich man now." He held the bags out.

Kormak took them. They were as heavy as ever. "This is what I carried all the way from the country of the light elves?"

"Yes."

"Won't the fey be angry with me?" Kormak asked.

"Yes. I suggest you go into the part of Ireland that the Norwegians and Danes have settled. You know their language. The fey have little power there."

Volund gestured down the grassy slope behind him. At the bottom, three horses grazed. "I will accompany you for a while. I would like to know my daughter. And the iron dog will make sure that no one bothers us."

They rode together into the part of Ireland the Norwegians held. The iron dog made sure they had no more adventures. Kormak bought a farm, and Alda stayed with him, as did Volund for a while. Kormak had more questions to ask him. How had Volund known to be in the tunnel when Kormak and Svanhild came riding? Was it an accident that Svanhild and Kormak were traveling together, or was that part of Volund's plan? How far back did the elf prince's planning go? To the elf who opened the door in the cliff and beckoned Kormak in?

But Volund grew silent and refused to answer these questions, except to say two things. "I plan deeply and slowly, as the story of Nidhad tells you. The king thought I was reconciled to life in the smithy, and he thought I was safe. I was not."

In addition, he said, "Not everything is planned."

He spent most of his time with Alda, sitting by her loom and watching her weave, his withered legs stretched out in front of him, encased in iron. His hands, folded in his lap, were thick and strong. His face was worn. Though elves aged slowly, he was obviously not young.

Of all the people Kormak had met — Egil, the lord of the light elves, the chiefs of the dark elves, the queen of the fey — Volund was the most formidable.

Sometimes he talked about the swords he had made. All were famous. More often he listened to Alda talk about her childhood. She never talked about her long stay in the land of the fey.

In the end, Volund went back into the lands of magic. Before he left, he said to Alda, "If you ever want to visit Elfland, send the iron dog to find me. He will always know where I am."

The dog growled. Volund touched it, and it suddenly looked like an ordinary wolfhound. "Stay here, Elding."

The dog said:

> *"Decent behavior*
> *outshines silver.*
> *Kindness is better*
> *than gold or fame.*

> *"Glad am I*
> *to be a farm dog,*
> *guarding the farmer,*
> *guarding the sheep."*

"I don't intend to raise sheep," Kormak said, scratching the dog behind its ears.

"Nonetheless, I will guard you and Alda," the dog growled.

Volund rode away.

"A hard man to understand," Alda said. "I'm glad he's gone."

"I wish he had answered more of my questions," Kormak replied.

Kormak raised horses and sold them at a good price. Alda wove. Her cloth became well known among the Norwegian and Danish settlers. Noble women, whose husbands had grown rich through raiding, bought it. Kormak and Alda had no children, but the wars in Ireland produced many orphans. They found several to foster. Kormak lived thirty years more, aging slowly and remaining strong. Alda did not age at all.

At last, Kormak grew sick and took to his bed. "What will you do?" he asked Alda.

"Go to Elfland," she replied. "The dog will know the way. Our foster children can have the farm and the silver that remains. I still have the gold bracelet and the gold and ivory broach, though I have never worn either. I want to return them to Volund."

"Have you ever regretted staying here?" Kormak asked.

"I have liked it better than the country of the fey," Alda replied. "As for Elfland, I will find out how I like it."

Alda sat beside Kormak until he died. After he was buried, she picked out a horse. "The farm is yours," she told her foster children. "I am taking this horse and the dog."

The children — grown men and women — begged her to stay.

"I want to see my father and the lands of my kin," she replied. "The dog will guard me."

And she rode away. •

THE BLACK SCHOOL

IN 1072 SAEMUNDUR SIGFUSSON left Iceland. At the time he was a lad of seventeen, tall and well built, with fair hair and blue eyes as bright and clear as a midsummer sky. His usual expression was calm and alert, and this told something about his personality.

He traveled with two other boys, Kalfur Arnason and Half-dan Einarsson. All three came from farms, since Iceland had no cities or towns. This doesn't mean the country suffered from the idiocy of rural life. As a group Icelanders have never been idiots; and many living in this period had traveled widely, going all over Europe and as far east as Constantinople. Some were learned, and more than a few were quick-witted. This last was especially true of Saemundur, as this story will demonstrate.

The boys went to Norway, then south to Paris. The journey was long and not entirely safe. The age of the Vikings was coming to an end. King Harald of Norway had died six years before in the Battle of Stamford Bridge, and a French duke ruled in England. There would be no more great invasions from the north. But sea robbers still remained in the coves of Europe and on the open ocean, as the boys knew. There were plenty of Icelanders who had done well as Vikings and come home to be prosperous and well-respected farmers.

Traveling on a Norwegian ship, they were less worried about Icelanders and Norwegians than Danes, Swedes, and Frisians. However, they reached France without incident. Their plan was to attend the university in Paris. All three were determined to get a college education, which was not possible in Iceland.

To us now, Paris then would seem a miserable village, full of low buildings and narrow, winding, muddy streets. All the famous landmarks — churches, palaces, fortresses, and bridges — lay in the future. To the three farm boys, however, it seemed huge and more full of people than the Althing, the annual meeting which was Iceland's greatest gathering. They had no idea where the university was. None knew any French. They did know Latin, but the people they met didn't understand them.

It was November by this time, a gray day with a fine rain falling. The early autumn evening was approaching rapidly. They had no money for an inn. What were they going to do?

As they wondered and glanced at one another, a voice spoke in their own language. "What are three Icelanders doing here?"

They looked toward the sound and saw a tall, handsome man in dark clothing. His hair and eyes were coal black. A long, black mustache drooped around his mouth. His face was so ruddy that it seemed to glow with reflected firelight — though there was no fire around, only the dim day and misty rain.

They had come to attend school, Saemundur replied. He was the boldest and most forthcoming of the three and served as their usual spokesman. But they hadn't been able to find the university among all these muddy, crooked streets.

"You're lucky to have found me," the man said. "The school is nearby. I'll lead you to it."

Off he went, wading through the muck in thick-soled shoes. They followed, happy to have found a guide, especially an Icelander. At length they came to a wall made of worn red bricks. In the middle was a door of black wood, bound with iron. Above the door, written in Latin, was:

You can learn much, if you enter here;
And lose much, if you don't take care.

"That doesn't sound good to me," said Kalfur Arnason. He was the most timid of the three.

"All knowledge is dangerous, if learned by a fool and used unwisely," the man replied. "Look at the story of Eve and the tree. She was a fool, as was her husband, and all of humanity has suffered as a result. But if a scholar takes care and behaves wisely, what he learns in this place will be of great use."

"I thought the university would be more imposing," said Saemundur, looking at the brick wall. "Large and tall, like the king's hall in Norway, and made of something more majestic, either wide planks of wood or blocks of stone."

"This building was made by the Romans," the man replied. "They were mighty builders, who preferred brick to all other materials. The knowledge here is as old as Rome. As for the building's height — the knowledge here goes deep, to the roots of the Earth."

This struck Saemundur as a bit odd. Shouldn't knowledge rise toward heaven? But he had traveled a long way and wasn't going to turn back before he had an education. If the university seemed odd, he needed to remember that it was foreign. What did he know about France or the Romans, coming from the far northern edge of the world?

He straightened his shoulders, pushed back his sleeves, and pulled at the door. It swung open slowly, its hinges shrieking. Inside was a flight of stairs, going down.

"This isn't what I expected," said Kalfur.

"Deep roots," the man replied.

The three boys glanced at one another. Saemundur was tired, wet, and cold. The others must be the same, he thought. A building that was underground would not be likely to leak;

and whatever else might be said about the place, it seemed to be well heated. Warm air flowed out the door.

He straightened his shoulders a second time and began to walk down. After a moment, the other boys followed. The man came last, swinging the door shut.

They moved through utter darkness. But it was good to be out of the rain and into warmth. A roaring fire must be burning somewhere below. Saemundur continued down, keeping one hand on the wall and testing each step before he put his weight on it. The stairs were either brick or stone, he couldn't tell which, and worn by use. That fit his idea of the university, which was old and famous. Many students must have walked up and down here. As his eyes adjusted, he saw a dim red glow ahead of him.

Down and down he went, till the steps ended. Now he was on a level floor. Instead of the hearth fire he had expected, there were many small flames. They burned at waist height, apparently in midair.

That was strange! Kalfur and Halfdan reached the bottom of the stairs and stood behind him, so close that he could feel their breathing on his neck. Gradually, he made out the scene. They were in a room full of tables. Books lay on the tabletops, and flames rose from their pages. The writing itself was burning, though the pages remained smooth and white. Men in dark robes leaned over the books, reading the fiery words.

"This is the school," said their guide.

"This cannot be the University of Paris," said Saemundur.

"It's called the Black School," said the man. "And you will remain here, till you have learned what's in these books. Believe me, the knowledge will do you far more good than what they teach at the university."

"I think you must be the devil," said Saemundur.

"That may or may not be," the man said. "But you're here for the time being. Make good use of the learning available!" Then he was gone, though they didn't know how.

After that, they did the obvious thing: climbed back up the stairs and tried the door. It was firmly shut and would not budge, no matter how hard they pushed.

Halfdan said, "This is not the way I expected my college education to begin."

"If we can't get out, then we must go down," said Saemundur. He led the way back to the room with the flaming books.

One of the readers looked up when they returned. His table was close to them, and the book in front of him burned brightly. They had no trouble making him out: a little fellow with a bent back and a long, sharp nose. Firelight gleamed in his large, pale eyes and on the drop of liquid that hung from his nose's tip. He wiped his nose with a sleeve, then spoke in Latin. "The door will not open till your education is complete."

"How will we know when that has happened?" Kalfur asked anxiously. "Are there teachers or tests?"

"The fiery books are your teachers. Whatever you want to know is in them or will appear, when you are ready. Study the books closely! Your only chance of escape lies with learning!

"There are no formal examinations. But we — the students here — test each other often. Every spring your guide, who is the school's provost, appears and announces who is ready to leave. When that happens, the people whose names are called race up the stairs. They are all afraid of being last. For the provost always takes the hindmost, though none of us knows where he takes him."

Looking around at the underground room, lit only by burning words, Saemundur could imagine where the last scholar was taken.

"How long are we likely to stay?" asked Kalfur.

"Three years or seven or, if you are like me, forever. I have a twisted foot as well as a bent back. If I ever graduate, I will certainly be the last scholar out the door. Knowing this, I have been careful not to learn too much."

"How will we live?" asked Halfdan. "Is there food down here? Or beds?"

"Both," the man said. He picked up the book in front of him and blew on the words. They flared up. His eyes glinted, as did the new drop which hung from his nose. "I'll show you the dormitory." Using the book as a lantern, he led the way.

They followed him into a narrow corridor. He had been telling the truth about his foot. He limped badly. They kept close, afraid of what the dark might hold. This was not cowardice, Saemundur told himself. Even a great warrior might fear darkness and the devil.

At length they came to a courtyard, surrounded by a colonnade. The ceiling — there had to be one — was far above them, hidden in shadow. In the court's middle a fountain spurted dark water. Around the edges, sheltered by the colonnade, were rooms.

"The ones with closed doors have current occupants. You can pick any with an open door." He led them to one of these. They looked in. The book's dim light revealed a bed of solid stone. A thin mattress lay on top. A stone ledge protruded by the opposite wall. "Most of us keep an open book on the ledge. It gives light, until you have learned enough to write fiery letters on the wall. Most are able to do that after a year or so."

Next he led them to a large room full of stone tables and benches. "This is the refectory. We gather here three times a day, if one can speak of 'day' in a place of continual dark. Hands come out of the walls, holding bowls of food and cups of beer. I've eaten better, but it is sustaining; and complaining does no good. The food will not improve."

They stayed in the hall. Other people joined them: men in

long robes, carrying books. Flames danced on the open pages. The books were laid down, but everyone remained standing.

Finally a bell rang. The low, dull sound vibrated through the floor, and the boys felt it in their bones and teeth. When the ringing ended, hands came out of the walls. They were troll-like, large and gray and hairy. Each held a bowl or cup.

"Take what you want," the bent man said. "But don't thank the providers. Above all, don't praise God or bless the food. It will make our providers angry, and they won't come for days."

The boys did as they were told, though it irked Saemundur to take without giving thanks. He was not an especially devout lad, being more in love with learning than religion; but he believed in courtesy.

The bowls held gray porridge. The beer was thin and bitter.

"We shall not grow fat here," Saemundur said. "But we have eaten worse at home during hard winters."

"Don't talk about home," said Halfdan. "It makes me long for blood sausage and pickled whale fat."

These were winter foods, served at feasts. Saemundur felt his mouth fill with saliva. But they weren't in Iceland or at a feast. He would have to eat what lay in front of him. The porridge was gritty and had little taste.

When they had finished, Saemundur asked where the scholars went to relieve themselves. He was badly in need of relief by this time. The bent man led them to a room with holes in the floor. The air smelled of urine and excrement. But the smell could have been much worse. Well, thought Saemundur, this was a place full of magic. Maybe magic was reducing the aroma.

They pissed and heard their urine hit far below. Maybe distance reduced the aroma, Saemundur thought. After they were done, they followed the bent man back to the dormitory.

"Pick three rooms in a row," he told them. "I'll leave my book on the floor outside, so you will have some light. The darkness here is hard to bear, especially at first."

Saemundur thanked him. "I want you to know who you have helped." He told the man their names and places of origin. "We all come from good families, well respected in Iceland, though it isn't likely you will recognize the names of our farmsteads."

"You seem like promising lads, worth helping," the man replied, and gave his name: Hermes. "It's a strange name for a man who can barely hobble. But my parents gave it to me, and I use it out of respect for them. I come from Germany, but have lived here in the school for many years."

The boys picked their rooms, and Hermes laid down the book. It glowed like a low fire. "Leave it untouched, even if you are curious, as clever lads usually are. Above all, don't look at the words. This is an advanced text, and the words it contains can be dangerous to beginners."

With this warning, the bent man left. The boys entered their cells. Sighing with weariness, Saemundur laid his bag on his room's stone ledge, then took off his cloak and laid it next to the bag. His sword and belt went on the cloak. He was too tired to think of undressing further. Instead he lay down on the stone bed. He soon discovered he couldn't sleep. The warm air had become stifling, and it was hard to decide what he found more disturbing — the darkness of the place or the book that was his only illumination. Red light came through the room's open door, dancing over rough stone walls.

He got up finally, got his sword, lay down again with the sword next to him, and considered his future. He was not the most religious lad who had ever lived in Iceland, but he wanted no dealings with the devil.

Men became famous and gained respect through honorable behavior and loyalty to family and friends. "Bare is the back with no brother behind it," the old saying told him. The devil had been an angel once, kin to the rest of God's servants. How well had he protected his brother angels? Compared to Grettir Asmundarson's brother Illugi, to give only one example, the devil was a disloyal coward. Illugi had died in defense of his brother, who was no prize, but kin. As a result, he was known and praised throughout Iceland. What had the devil ever done that was noble or brave?

Nonetheless, Saemundur was stuck in this place; and though he admired heroes like Illugi and Grettir, he had no desire to make a last stand. He would bide his time and learn what he could.

At length, he fell asleep. But his sleep was restless, often broken and troubled by bad dreams. When he woke the last time, the bent man was back. "I have brought you each a book," he said. "They are beginners' texts, which will not teach you anything too harmful, and they will serve as lanterns."

Saemundur rose and washed himself in the courtyard fountain.

"The servants here are trolls, as you may have suspected," Hermes said. "If you need anything cleaned or mended, put it outside your door. The trolls will come while you sleep, collect it, and bring it back. Never thank them; and never try to see them. They are shy and ungracious."

This struck Saemundur as wrong. But Hermes knew more than he did about the school.

They visited the privy, then went to breakfast, using their books to light the way. Once again, the food was porridge and bitter beer.

"I was told the food in Paris was fine, far better than we have in Iceland," Halfdan grumbled. "How can a man achieve anything notable with fodder like this?"

"We will do as we must," Saemundur replied.

———

So began three years of study. First they read the books Hermes had brought them, which were Latin grammars, since Latin was the language of magic and theirs could be improved, according to the bent man. "You may think it's a trivial mistake to use the wrong declension, but if you do it in a spell, especially a spell that raises a demon — ."

After they finished with the grammars, they moved to the books that lay on the tables. The school was full of these, room after room: history and natural history, philosophy, alchemy, astronomy, all the sciences taught by words that blazed and flickered.

All three were in love with learning. It was hard to live in darkness and fear of the devil, but the books were a consolation. "We would never have learned this much in Iceland," they told each other. "Knowledge like this is worth a little suffering."

In time, they came to know the other scholars. Some were likable, others were not. The bent man seemed the best of the lot, always friendly and full of information. He was never rude to anyone, not even the trolls. But he did not seem especially impressed by the school or its scholars or even its master. This was strange, since he was trapped in the school. His attitude must be due to courage and a natural good humor. The Icelandic lads found it reassuring. If he could face a lifetime in the dark without complaint, they could face three or seven years.

At the end of a year, the provost appeared and summoned everyone to the room at the foot of the stairs. This time he was dressed in a scarlet robe. A red hat rested on his head, and a gold broach gleamed on the hat. His face was as ruddy as ever. They had no trouble seeing him, because the books in the room burned more brightly in his presence. Every table flared with red fire.

He named the graduates in a ringing voice. Those he named waited till he was done. Then, when he fell silent, all raced for the stairs, scrambling up, pushing and shoving. As the last graduate ran past the provost, he reached out and grabbed. The man screamed. Both vanished.

"That was certainly a remarkable sight," Saemundur commented. "I wonder why anyone continues to study after seeing it, and why the graduates wait till every name is called."

"Only one man a year is lost," Hermes said. "Everyone thinks he will escape. Another will stumble or be slow. And they must wait till every name is called. That is the rule."

They went back to studying. But Saemundur began to consider how they were going to survive their graduation day.

One morning, midway through the second year, Saemundur was in the privy, pissing into a hole. A voice rose up to him. "Could you please stop that, Saemundur Sigfusson? I'm down here cleaning, and I don't appreciate the falling liquid."

Surprise made his urination cease.

"Thank you," said the voice. "This work is difficult enough, without having piss fall on me."

"You gave me thanks," said Saemundur.

"Of course I did. I ought to have the right to live and work without being pissed on. But here, in this place, only courtesy keeps urine from raining down on me."

"I was told you hated courtesy, and I should never thank you."

"Lies," said the voice below him. "Or ignorance. Few of the scholars here bother to learn about those who serve them."

"In that case, thank you for the food you have served me and my comrades. It could have been better tasting, but it kept us alive. And thank you for the cleaning and mending."

"You're welcome," said the voice. "I'm out of the way now. You can continue pissing."

After that, Saemundur always called out before he used the privy holes. Most often, no one replied. But a few times, a voice said, "Wait a bit, Saemundur," which he always did. In addition, he began to thank the gray hands when they came out of the refectory wall, holding cups and bowls of food. He spoke quietly, so the other scholars didn't hear him. A wise man doesn't draw attention.

His food improved. It wasn't anything the other scholars would notice: beer with a better flavor, porridge with less grit, meat with less gristle. Now and then, he got butter with the porridge or a cup of wine.

His two companions did notice, since they ate with him every day.

"What's going on?" Halfdan asked.

Saemundur told his secret.

"If that's all that's necessary, I can be polite as well," said Halfdan.

"I never thought trolls were so sensitive," Kalfur remarked.

"No one likes neglect," Saemundur replied. "I should have realized this sooner."

One night he woke from sleep and heard a noise outside his door. He picked up the book he was studying and flipped it open, then opened the door.

A huge, gray creature was hunched over the clothes he'd left for mending. As far as he could tell, it was naked. Its skin was rough and pebbly; its brows beetled; its nose was long and bulbous. Gray hair like old hay covered its head. It turned and looked at him with a tiny, beady eye. "Well, Saemundur Sigfusson, how do you like what you see?"

"The devil is handsome," Saemundur replied. "Which tells me that I should not rely overmuch on good looks. And though you may not be the best looking of folk, you've done no harm to me. More than that, you have cared for me and my comrades."

"Not willingly," said the troll. "We'd sooner be where we belong, inside cliffs and mountains. But the devil holds us prisoner and forces us to work for him."

"Willingly or not, you have done me good," Saemundur said.

The troll hunched its shoulders, looking uncomfortable. Hermes was right. These folk were shy.

"Don't think we're your friends," the troll said. "We have an old quarrel with humanity. The world was far more peaceful before it filled with people. We are grateful that you no longer piss on us. But how far our gratitude goes is not certain. Nor can we do much, since we are prisoners and slaves."

"Thank you for the warning," Saemundur said.

The troll ducked its head, then gathered up his clothing and left. It moved remarkably quickly for something so large and rocklike. In a moment, it was gone.

Saemundur went back to bed. He was certain the troll was telling the truth: the servants here would not be able to help him and might not be willing to, even if they could. This was to be expected. Neither trolls nor elves had ever been friends to humankind. The best one could hope for from either was lack of malice.

The second year passed, though Saemundur could not say whether it went by quickly or slowly. Time was hard to judge in a place without day and night or seasons. How he missed the long days of Iceland's summers, when the sun barely sank below the mountains! Even the Icelandic winter, with its brief daylight, was better than unending dark.

The only way to measure time was the meals, which happened at regular intervals. The students had given these names, which reminded them of life outside the school. One was "breakfast" and always porridge. After it came the "midday meal," a strange name for a place without daylight. This was usually dry bread and hard cheese. The last meal was "supper," either meat or fish. The meat was usually tough, and the fish preserved in some way, dried, salted, or pickled. The Icelanders had no objection to preserved fish, but it was better done at home.

Was this the best the devil could do? they asked one another in quiet voices. What did this say about his power? Or his hospitality? After the trolls took a liking to them, they ate better than the other students, but not so well as to make them forget the food in Iceland.

Most of the students went to bed after supper, though some studied. Hermes warned them this was dangerous. "The books are seductive, and there's nothing here to remind one of nature and natural behavior. It's easy to lose track and forget to eat and sleep. Then, when you graduate, you will be too weak to run. Eat regularly, sleep regularly, exercise regularly, and watch one another to make sure none of you is becoming lost in the books."

The Icelanders consulted and decided on three forms of exercise. Most important was climbing the stairs that led from the school to daylight. They did this slowly at first, then worked up to a brisk walk, and finally to a run. Each time they reached the top, they tried the door. It was always locked.

They wrestled, a sport they had learned in Iceland, and explored the school. This last was done for two reasons: to exercise and to look for a second way out.

The rooms went on and on. Those close to the stairs and dormitory were usually occupied by one or two or three students. Many books lay open on the stone tables, and the boys could see well enough.

As they moved farther from the stairs, there were fewer students, and most of the books were closed. A dim red glow seeped out between the shut covers, not enough to light the rooms. The Icelanders were reluctant to open the books they found. Who could say what hellfire was contained inside?

Instead they brought their own reading material: small primers on harmless topics, such as herbs. The light these shed was not intense, but they were able to see what the rooms contained: stone tables, stone walls, closed books, dust.

Once they found a dead man on the floor of a far distant room. His body had dried to dark skin over bones. The remnants of a scholar's robe covered him partially.

"A student, apparently," Saemundur remarked. "He must have lost track of time — or the way back to the dormitory."

"Or opened the wrong book," Kalfur added uneasily.

Halfdan said, "It seems to me the trolls could do a better job of cleaning."

Farther on, they found a disarticulated skeleton, its bones piled neatly on a table. The skull rested on top, staring at them with empty eyeholes.

"This fellow looks neater than the last one," said Halfdan. "But he could be cleaned away entirely."

A deep voice spoke out of the wall. "Don't question our work. We have our orders."

Halfdan apologized for being critical.

"It doesn't seem as if these rooms will ever end, and we're finding nothing useful by our exploration," Kalfur put in.

"There is no second way out, if that's what you are looking for," the voice in the wall said. "If there were, we would have taken it years ago."

"Thank you for the information," said Saemundur.

After that, they confined their exercise to wrestling and stair climbing.

At the end of the second year, the provost came again and called them all together. This time he wore black leggings and a bright red tunic, fastened with a gold belt. His shoes were red leather. Gold rings adorned his fingers, which were thick and fleshy, black hair growing thickly on their backs. He called out the names of those who were graduating. As each name was called, Saemundur looked at the student. Most seemed caught between hope and fear. No question what they were thinking. *Ah, to finally leave this place! But what if I am last?*

At length, the provost fell silent. The graduates ran for the stairs. The first to reach them was a wiry Italian. Saemundur had often seen him running through the school's rooms and around the dormitory courtyard, exercising as Hermes had advised. Far above the man, sunlight shone through the school's open door. The Italian raced toward it, touching every other step. The others scrambled after him but could not keep up. The distance between them grew wider, till suddenly — Saemundur did not see how it happened — the Italian tripped and fell. He sprawled full length over the stairs, clearly stunned. The other graduates reached him, going past and over. One — the last — kicked him as he tried to rise, though this might have been an accident.

The Italian staggered to his feet, looking dazed. The kick had been to his head. The others were all past him, pelting up the stairs, their long scholar robes fastened high. He looked after them, obviously thinking of following.

"No," the provost called.

The Italian turned and saw the provost, holding out a fleshy hand, gold rings gleaming in the light of the books. His face paled, and he glanced around wildly. All the remaining students — those who would not graduate this year — stood motionless and silent. Most were looking down. But Saemundur forced himself to look into the doomed man's eyes. They were wide with fear, the dark irises rimmed with white.

This was no kin of his, Saemundur thought. Nor a friend. Not even a countryman. There was no reason for him to risk his life.

The Italian laughed harshly, a sound of despair, and came

slowly down the stairs. He took the provost's hand. As he did so, a scream burst from his mouth. A cry of utter horror and fear, it seemed to Saemundur. The two vanished, still clasping hands.

"So much for exercise," said Halfdan.

Kalfur groaned.

Saemundur drew a deep breath. The Italian had been a brave man, though obviously unlucky. "We have no reason to believe that will happen to us," he said. "But exercise may not be enough."

What else was there? He asked Hermes, adding that he was not entirely happy that he'd kept still while the Italian met his fate. "Though I owed him nothing," he added.

"It is not easy to oppose the devil," the bent man said. "He's not clever, but he does have considerable power. You will discover how much in the next year, when you read his great books of sorcery."

"I've always heard the devil is cunning," Saemundur protested.

"Men like to believe so," the bent man replied. "Because they want someone to blame for their behavior. It's easier to say they have been tricked by a master of trickery, a great and splendid being of surpassing subtlety and guile, than to admit that they were led into evil by their own failings. Greed, meanness, selfishness, laziness, and lack of imagination — these are the traits that lead us all to evil, even the devil. It was not cleverness that brought him to hell, but pettiness. How clever can a being be, who was an angel and gave up that bliss to grovel in excrement?"

"The provost doesn't look shitty to me," said Saemundur cautiously.

"He wears red clothing and gold. Does that impress you so much? He is able to play simple tricks on the ignorant, as he did when he led you and your friends — three foreign boys who knew nothing about Paris — to this place. But he cannot lead you into evil. You must chose evil for yourselves."

Saemundur looked at the bent man with curiosity. How did he know so much about the devil?

Hermes laughed and did not explain.

In their third year, the three Icelanders began to study the devil's books of sorcery. They lay among the other books on the tables but were unusually large and heavy, bound with black leather and iron. Most were closed, and it was difficult to lift the covers. Indeed, it seemed the books were resisting them. But a strong, quick tug would get most open.

The pages inside were black with bright illuminations. Elaborate initial letters began each chapter, shining like jewels in firelight; and vines ran up the margins, adorned with flowers whose petals flicked like so many flames. Where chapters ended and there was a little space, the Icelanders found paintings. They had never seen anything so well-done and lifelike, nor anything so lovely and rich.

Tiny lords and ladies danced and banqueted. Warriors fought. Hunters pursued elk, boar, bear, and deer. Everyone looked prosperous and handsome.

Exhaling in wonder, the Icelanders began to read. There were no stools, and the books could not be lifted from the tables, so they read standing. This was good, they found. Sore feet kept them from forgetting where they were, and reminded them when it was time to leave. They worked together, always remaining in the same room. If one became too preoccupied, the others would rouse him and take him off to exercise, eat, and sleep.

Saemundur learned the most quickly, though the others were not far behind him. It was not entirely pleasant work. The spells in the books were often disturbing. But the pictures were a comfort. At times, when he could bear the spells no longer, Saemundur would turn the pages, looking for another lovely image.

One time when he was doing this, he came to a painting of a dragon, asleep on its hoard of gold. The work was so fine that he could see the slow movement of the animal's side as it breathed in and out.

The dragon lifted its head. Saemundur jerked back in surprise. A small, bright eye opened. The dragon regarded him.

You will be free in another year, said a whisper in his mind. *But still a farm boy from Iceland, unless you study well. What you learn now can lead to wealth and power.*

The whispering ceased. The dragon was motionless, its head still lifted and its bright eye open.

Saemundur drew a deep breath and turned the page, finding another scene: a king on his throne, dressed in scarlet, a gold crown on his head. Leaning forward, he peered at the tiny face. It bore his features. He was the royal man.

Is this not what you want? the whisper asked.

Saemundur paged ahead. There he was again, dancing with a woman so rich and beautiful she must be a queen; there again with councilors; and there on a horse, among mounted retainers.

Farther on, he found himself in the black robe of a scholar, summoning demons with a broad gesture. They hurried toward him: little red mannequins bent over by the weight of what they carried — boxes full of rings and broaches, fine swords and axes, gold belts and chains, food befitting a royal banquet. Staring at a roast goose, so well painted that he could smell it, Saemundur groaned with desire.

Is this not what you want? the whisper repeated.

Saemundur closed the book. What *did* he want? he asked himself, resting his hands on the book's black cover.

To go home.

The whisper hissed in his mind, sounding unhappy.

Here was the dilemma, Saemundur told himself. To graduate, he had to learn these books. To remain his own man, he had to resist their seductions. How could he manage this in a dark, impoverished place, without the ordinary pleasures that would remind him who he was and why he loved his life?

He walked back to the dormitory, through rooms full of scholars and brightly burning books.

That evening, he spoke to Halfdan and Kalfur. "I propose that we meet every night and talk about Iceland. Let's remind each other of the lives we used to lead and want to lead again. This will help us resist the devil's seductions."

"Well," said Halfdan. "I want the girl on the next farm, Thordis. She has long, thick, fair hair and bright blue eyes; and her father is able to give her a good dowry. She promised to wait for me. When I become a priest, as I expect to do, she'll be a good and noble wife."

Kalfur leaned against the stone wall and closed his eyes. "I miss the smell of hay in the fields and the taste of cod, fresh from the ocean; and I'd like to go riding up the valley behind our farm on my horse Hlaupar. He's dun colored with a black mane and tail, and his gait is so smooth that I can sit on his back and drink ale without spilling a drop. Not that I'll be drinking while riding up the valley. Better to be sober and see the mountains clearly!"

Saemundur thought awhile. Women were fine, though he wasn't interested in any one in particular. Horses were fine. Nothing could compare with the sight of mountains under a midsummer sky or the ocean gleaming in the winter's half light. But it seemed as if he missed ordinary things the most. "I'd like a decent loaf of bread," he said finally, "warm from the oven, and some decent cheese to go with the bread, and some puffin eggs."

The creature in his mind hissed angrily.

After that, they did as Saemundur had proposed, meeting every night to talk about their homes.

The third year approached its end. "I think the three of you are going to graduate," Hermes told Saemundur. "You might consider how you are going to get out the door safely."

"I have a plan that ought to work," Saemundur replied. "But I haven't thought of a way to get you up the stairs. It seems cowardly and unmanly to leave you behind, after all your help."

Hermes smiled. "I don't want to leave."

"Why not?" asked Saemundur in amazement.

"There will be other young men in need of advice, and even a few young women. Do you think God allows the devil to go unopposed anywhere, even in hell?"

The bent man straightened till the crook in his back vanished. He stood taller than Saemundur now, his shoulders broad and his pale face handsome. His eyes stayed blue, though they seemed more brilliant than before, shining like ice in sunlight. Behind him, in the shadows, large wings unfolded, barred gray and white like the wings of an Icelandic falcon.

Saemundur's mouth dropped open, and his mind filled with questions. Was Hermes an angel? If so, why did he bear the name of a pagan god? And why had he told them the trolls could not bear gratitude? Was this a deliberate lie? Or was Hermes ignorant of the true nature of trolls? How could that be? Did God have ignorant servants?

Hermes raised a hand. "I can't answer all your questions, but I will give you two pieces of information. First, God is often subtle, but never malicious; and second, trolls cannot be trusted."

"Nonetheless, I will treat them with courtesy," Saemundur replied. "A man should always be courteous, unless he wants to start a fight."

Hermes tilted his head. It might have been agreement or not. "I want to give you a parting gift. It's small enough to hide in your clothes, and it may prove useful." He held out a small book.

Saemundur took it and opened it. Unlike the school's books, it did not flare and burn. Instead the black letters lay motionless on the white pages. That was comforting, after the devil's writhing words. He read a page or two. It was the Book of Psalms. That also was comforting. It reminded him of something Icelanders have always known: good poetry is more valuable than magic. It lasts longer and gives better fame, as the story of Egil Skallagrimsson showed. Egil was a magician, who drove the king of Norway out of Norway with a spell. But it was Egil's poetry that made him famous. Without it, he would simply have been another sorcerer, instead of the greatest skald who ever lived in Iceland.

Saemundur thanked Hermes. The angel smiled and stepped away, his back rebending, and the wings vanishing. Once again his face was sharp and ugly. A drop of liquid dangled from the tip of his long nose.

Several night later Saemundur woke to the sound of thuds. They seemed to come from the walls of his room. There were shouts as well, too muffled for him to make out words. The trolls, he thought. Why were they making so much noise?

The thudding grew so loud that his walls began to shake. The shouts seemed right next to him, though he still couldn't make out any words.

"I'm trying to sleep," he shouted finally.

The noise stopped, and he dozed off. Then he heard a new sound. Something was scratching on his door. Rising, he gathered his sword and a book to use for light. Flipping the book open with one hand, he opened the door. A troll sat outside. Its gray face was mottled with bruises. Its gray hair stood upright, as if pulled, and its long nose was swollen.

"We know you will be leaving soon," the troll said. "And we have decided to give you a parting gift, since you and your friends have thanked us for our work, as no one else here does; and you haven't pissed on us. That counts for a lot.

"Some of us wanted to give you one thing; some wanted to give you another. We had a vigorous discussion, which you may have heard. In the end, we decided to give you both things. Take these with our good wishes, though you should not expect us — or any of our kind — to help you again. The world was a much better place before people." The troll handed over two bags.

Saemundur took them with thanks, and the huge creature scuttled away with surprising speed. Once it was gone, he opened the bags. One held grains of salt, and the other held lumps of gold.

He went into his room and looked around at the walls. "Thank you," he said again.

"You are welcome," the walls replied. "To us, every rock and crystal and vein of metal is lovely. But we know your people value salt and gold."

The next morning, the provost appeared and called everyone to the bottom of the stairs.

Saemundur said to his friends, "If the devil calls our names, go up the stairs as quickly as you can and don't worry about me. I intend to follow after you. If the devil grabs any of us, it will be me. I have a plan to evade him."

The other two looked dubious, but did not argue.

He put the bent man's gift in his purse, along with the trolls' two gifts. His cloak went over his shoulders, but he did not fasten it or put his arms in the sleeves. He took nothing else except his sword, which he did not fasten on for fear of tripping over it. Instead he carried it — sheathed in its scabbard — in one hand.

The three friends went together to the stairs. The provost was there, as in previous years. This time his clothes were entirely red, except for a wide black belt. The buckle was gold and shaped like a sleeping dragon. The sword hanging at his side had a gold hilt shaped like a dragon's head, its eyes open and set with bloodred rubies.

How could Saemundur ever have imagined this was a mortal man? His eyes were black pits. His teeth — he was smiling — were square and white, like blocks of stone. Saemundur imagined them grinding men or women.

When everyone had gathered, the provost called out the graduates' names. All three of the Icelanders were on the list. They glanced at one another. Saemundur readied himself.

As soon as the devil fell silent, the graduates — all except Saemundur — raced for the stairs. An elbow caught Saemundur in the ribs. A shoe kicked him in the shin. He staggered. By the time he recovered, the others were on the stairs.

Well, he had planned to be last. He started after the others. The only route led past the provost, who reached out as Saemundur ran by. His fleshy, hairy hand grabbed the edge of Saemundur's cloak and yanked. As Saemundur had planned, the cloak fell off. The devil fell backward, and Saemundur ran up the stairs.

Exercise and fear made him quick. Nonetheless, he had not gone far when he heard the devil behind him. The red man's shoes must be shod in iron. They rang on the stairs like hammers beating on an anvil. Saemundur ran harder. Above him, sunlight poured through the school's open door, illuminating his fellow graduates as they scrambled upward.

"You won't escape," the devil called from below.

Saemundur kept climbing. He was getting closer to the other graduates. Before he caught up with them, though, they reached the upper landing and pushed through the door. A moment later, he was at the top of the stairs, gasping with effort. The doorway was empty. Beyond it, he saw fresh snow, marked by the footprints of fleeing scholars.

Almost at his heels, the devil said, "I always take the hindmost."

"One comes behind me," Saemundur gasped. "He is your rightful prey."

"Who?" asked the devil.

Saemundur pointed at the stone floor. His shadow lay there, sharp and black and solid looking.

Who can say what the devil saw? A scholar fallen on the landing? Some poor soul Saemundur had leaped over and left behind? Greedy and overhasty, the red man reached down. At the same moment, Saemundur stepped into the doorway. He could not get through it. Something was holding him back. He glanced around and saw the devil holding his shadow, pulling it — and him — into the school.

"No, you don't," cried Saemundur. In a single motion, he drew his sword and brought it down, cutting through his shadow where it met his feet. The shadow sprang free. With a shout of rage, the devil fell backward and tumbled down the stairs.

Saemundur stepped through the doorway. A bright, pale winter sun blazed in the middle of the clear blue sky. The snowy street was empty, except for Kalfur and Halfdan.

"What next?" asked Halfdan.

"Let's go home," said Saemundur. "I've had enough of French education."

———

They found a goldsmith and sold the nuggets Saemundur got from the trolls. All three had purses full of money after that, and the money — pieces of silver and copper — would be easier to spend than gold. Then they bought horses. They were bigger than Icelandic horses and did not look as hardy or intelligent.

Halfdan and Kalfur made disapproving noises.

"They will have to do," said Saemundur. "I'm not going to walk to Iceland."

It was midafternoon, but they were not willing to stay in Paris any longer. Instead they started across the wide plain west of the city. Nothing worth noting happened for several days. The weather was cold enough to keep snow on the ground, but not any colder. They slept outside. Three young men with horses and swords were not likely to be robbed.

After four or five days, Halfdan said, "Someone is following us."

Saemundur nodded. "And keeping up with us, though he's on foot. I'm almost certain it's the provost."

Kalfur groaned.

"I'll go and talk with him," Saemundur said. "He can't have much power in broad daylight, and he has something I'd like to get back."

The other lads argued, but Saemundur was adamant. Finally, they let him go. He turned his horse, riding till he reached the man on foot. Sure enough, it was the devil, striding along in boots caked with winter mud. A black cloak covered him. If he wore any gold or silver, it wasn't visible.

"Couldn't you afford a horse?" Saemundur asked.

"Most animals dislike me," the devil said, glaring up at Saemundur. "You cheated me. I'm not willing to let you get away with it."

Saemundur considered this while stroking his horse's neck. The animal was clearly unhappy to be so close to the devil.

Maybe these foreign horses were more intelligent than he had previously thought. "I'll make you a bargain," he said finally. "Come after me tonight, while I'm sleeping. If you can seize me — well, then, you will have me. If not, I want my shadow back."

The devil frowned and muttered, then agreed. Saemundur rejoined his companions.

That evening, they stopped at a farmhouse. It was barely more than a hut, but there was a shed for the horses and room in the shed for the Icelanders to sleep beside their animals. The farmer was a poor man, ragged and unkempt, as ugly as a troll. "I can offer you shelter, but the year has been hard, and my lord is greedy. I don't even have food for myself and my wife."

"We have brought our own food," Halfdan said, "and will share it with you in return for our night's shelter."

"I need two things, which you are likely to have," Saemundur put in. "A bowl and water to put in it."

"I have several bowls, and one — the best — is neither chipped nor cracked. As for water, there is a stream behind the house."

Saemundur took the bowl and filled it with water, then sprinkled the trolls' salt in.

They spread their food out. The householder joined them, along with his bony, ragged wife. They ate as if they hadn't seen food for days. Most likely they had not. Things were better in Iceland, Saemundur thought. Their hosts there would have been farmers with their own sheep and cattle, not people like these, who seemed little better than slaves. Though there were poor farmers in Iceland, he admitted to himself after a moment, and beggars as well. If he ever had a farm, he would make sure that poor folk and travelers were well fed.

The Icelanders retired to the shed. Kalfur and Halfdan piled up hay to make a bed. Saemundur lay on the dirt floor, the bowl of salt water on his chest. Soon they were all asleep. Saemundur dreamed that he was dead. His body drifted in the wide ocean, animals swimming around him: whales and seals and cod with golden eyes. Some of the cod were gray as silver. Others were red as copper. The devil was above him in an open boat, desperately rowing and shouting as he rowed. "I know you're down there, Saemundur. I'll find you. You won't escape me a second time."

But the animals swimming around Saemundur hid him, and the night passed as it began: Saemundur drifting in the ocean current, the devil rowing and shouting above him.

In the morning, the three Icelanders went on their way. Saemundur gave the farmer a silver coin and thanks for use of the bowl. "It proved very useful."

The morning was bright and passed without trouble. Around noon clouds blew in, turning the sky iron gray. A few hard grains of snow came down, whirling in a sharp wind. Halfdan said, "That old troublemaker is behind us again."

"I'll talk to him," Saemundur said, and turned his horse.

It was the devil, of course, tramping along in boots thick with mire. "You tricked me, Saemundur," he said. "And I won't return your shadow."

"Let's try a second time," Saemundur replied. "If you can find me tonight, I'll be yours. If not, I want my shadow."

"I never imagined you'd learn so much in my school," the devil said in a surly tone.

"That's the danger of education," Saemundur said. "If you give people the chance to learn, who can say what will happen?"

The devil snarled. Saemundur rode back to his companions.

That evening they found another farmhouse. The farmer was better fed than their first host. Instead of a worn, old wife, he had a sprightly son. Dinner was duck with root vegetables.

When they were done eating, Saemundur asked to borrow the wood trencher for the night.

"That's an odd request," the sprightly son commented.

"Nothing is odd, when a paying guest asks for it," his father replied, and handed the trencher to Saemundur. A small pool of grease lay in the bottom, a mixture of blood and fat. "Do you want that cleaned out?" their host asked.

"No," said Saemundur and took the trencher outside. The night was cold and still. A full moon shone. He had no trouble seeing the road in front of the house, churned up by cartwheels and hooves. Ice shone in the cart ruts. A small, bare bush cast a sharp-edged, spiny shadow. Saemundur gathered a lump of frozen dirt and set it in the trencher, pressing it down into the pool of grease. After that, he broke two twigs off the bush and tied them together with a bit of thread from his shirt, making a cross. He stuck the cross into the clod of dirt and went back inside.

The farmer and his son looked at the trencher, and the son opened his mouth. "A fool speaks and shows his folly," the father said. "A silent man is considered wise."

The house had a spare room. The Icelanders went there. As before, Halfdan and Kalfur took the bed, which was a real bed this time. Saemundur lay on the floor, the wood trencher on his chest. The room was warm. The clod of dirt thawed, soaking up the grease. The tiny cross cast a tiny shadow, until Halfdan put out their lamp.

Saemundur went to sleep and dreamed he was buried in a graveyard. A wood cross rose from his grave, and a wood fence surrounded the graveyard. The devil stood outside the fence.

"How did you manage to get here?" he asked Saemundur. "You were alive this afternoon, unless that was your ghost I spoke to. And why are you buried in holy ground, where I can't reach you?"

Saemundur kept quiet. If he opened his mouth to defend himself, the devil would know he was alive. Better to keep his lips pressed together, while the devil paced along the fence, taunting and threatening. Holy ground could not protect him, the devil cried. He was doomed and damned. His only hope was to swear allegiance to the devil. Then he would be a housecarl in hell, instead of a miserable, tormented slave.

This was not enough of a temptation. Saemundur remained silent. At dawn the devil vanished, and Saemundur woke.

The three Icelanders ate breakfast, then continued west. Late in the afternoon Kalfur said, "The old problem remains with us."

Saemundur sighed and turned back. Here came the devil in a long, black cloak, blowing on his icy hands as his tall boots climbed over the cart ruts.

"I am still missing my shadow," Saemundur said.

"You are still cheating me," the devil replied.

Saemundur sighed again. "One more time. If you can manage to get me tonight, my soul is yours. If not, I want my shadow."

The devil agreed with a curt nod. Saemundur returned to his companions. That evening they found a third farmhouse. It was better built than the previous two. A tall, handsome woman greeted them at the door. "My husband is laid up with a bad cold," she said. "But I can give you lodging, so long as you behave yourselves."

The three Icelanders swore they were harmless. "Though I have a request that may seem odd," Saemundur added.

The woman frowned. "What?"

"A few coals out of your fire and a bowl to contain them."

The woman looked at him closely, then nodded and said, "You may need the coals more than I do," a remark that seemed cryptic to all of them.

They ate dinner and drank ale, served by the woman and watched by a large, fierce-looking dog. When they were done, the woman brought a metal bowl and scooped glowing coals into it. "There you are," she said to Saemundur. "Use it carefully."

Saemundur promised he would.

They retired to their room, which had two large beds. Kalfur and Halfdan offered to share, but Saemundur insisted on the floor. He folded a piece of cloth and put it on his chest, laying the bowl on top. It was hot and might burn him, if he didn't have protection. Then he went to sleep and dreamed he was in hell. This was not the old hell of his ancestors, ice cold and full of poisonous snakes. Instead it was the modern place, where sinners roasted on beds of coal, poked by little demons with long roasting forks.

Saemundur lay like all the others, coals burning his backside, while the demons stabbed his arms, legs, chest, and belly. The pain was agonizing. Even worse was the thought that he would be here forever, burning and twisting, while the little red demons laughed.

In the distance he heard the devil calling. "Saemundur, where are you? I'll find you this time, no matter where you have hidden yourself."

One of the demons plunged his fork deep into Saemundur's belly. The Icelander howled.

"I heard that," the devil said. "I have you now!"

The fork twisted inside Saemundur, and he gave a second howl.

"Why, you're in hell," cried the devil. "Why am I looking for you in France?"

Saemundur howled a third time as the demon yanked his guts out. They hung in loops from the demon's fork like so many sausages, gleaming with fat and blood.

The devil appeared by Saemundur's bed of coals and laughed in triumph. "Ha! Aha!"

A moment later, Saemundur woke. His whole body ached, and he felt a burning sensation in his midriff. It was the bowl, he realized. It had slid off the folded cloth and lay on his bare belly. The hot metal was burning his skin, he didn't know how badly, but the pain seemed trivial compared to the pain of hell. Groaning softly, he lifted the bowl and set it on the floor.

The room's door opened. Their hostess strode in, carrying a lamp. "What kind of guest are you? The devil has been wandering through my house, calling your name. He would have come into my bedroom, except for my fierce dog. I can't have my husband bothered like this. He's a sick man."

Saemundur sat up carefully. "How do you know the devil is here? Are you a witch?"

"No, but my husband is a sorcerer. The devil cursed him, so he's never well, but goes from one illness to another. Thus far, I have been able to keep him alive with the help of garlic soup and my good fierce dog, who barks whenever the devil comes near."

Saemundur looked at his companions, who were still fast asleep.

"The dog is my husband's dog, or was till he got sick. It's magical. I and my husband can hear it bark, but no one else."

"Ah," said Saemundur and climbed to his feet. "That explains why I didn't hear the dog, though the devil's voice was clear enough, even at a distance. I heard every word he spoke."

The woman looked at the floor behind Saemundur. "I realized there was something strange about you, when you came in. Now I see what it is. You have no shadow."

"The devil stole it, and I have been in a contest with him to win it back."

"You'll never win. He cheats."

"He says I cheat," Saemundur replied.

"Do you?"

"I use the magic he taught me."

"Then you are cheating. Everything about him is a lie. He promised my husband many things, but all he gave him was bad luck and illness."

"You helped me, by giving me the bowl and the coals," Saemundur said. "Is there anything I can do to help your husband?"

"Come and see him and decide."

The woman led Saemundur to another room. The window shutters were closed, keeping out moonlight. The only illumination was the lamp the woman carried. Its dim flicker allowed Saemundur to see the man on the bed. He had thrown the blanket off and lay in a long shirt, damp with sweat: a tall man with big bones, very thin. Strange protrusions grew from every part of his body, like fungus on a dying tree. They were the same pale color as his skin.

The fierce dog lay next to the bed, watching Saemundur with pale eyes.

"The growths will vanish in a day or two," the woman said, "and be replaced with some other kind of sickness — a heavy cough or nose bleed, loose bowels, palsy, sneezing, a tic. Not all at once, but one after another, intermixed with diseases I have never seen nor heard of and cannot easily describe."

"This magic is beyond me," Saemundur said. "I can think of only one thing that might help. Make a cross and lay it on your husband's chest over his heart."

"He does not believe in Christ."

Saemundur thought for a moment. "In that case, take a hammer and lay it on your husband's chest. I can't do this, since I intend to be a Christian priest. But if your husband won't ask

Christ for help, then he will have to turn to other gods; and the old stories say Thor is a friend to men."

"Who is Thor?" asked the woman.

Saemundur looked at her, surprised by her ignorance. "One of the old gods, who ruled the north before Christ came. I don't know how much power he has in this age and country. But I can't think of anyone else."

"My husband doesn't believe in any god."

"That doesn't seem wise, especially if he believes in the devil."

"It's the way he is," the woman said firmly.

"Then I have no more advice."

The next morning the Icelanders went on their way. Glancing back, Saemundur saw the devil trudging behind them, a dark figure amid falling snow. He was tired of the contest. He had defeated the devil three times and still did not have his shadow. The woman at the farmhouse was right. Everything the red man did was a trick.

They reached the coast and sold their horses, then took a ship for Norway. The weather was mild and their journey unremarkable, except for the large seal that accompanied them day after day.

"The devil?" asked Kalfur.

"Yes," said Saemundur glumly. "He doesn't give up easily. I don't want another contest with him, but maybe I will have to."

Their ship docked at Trondheim, and they went to pay their respects to the bishop. He was busy at this time, since construction had started on the Nidaros Cathedral, which would be the finest church in Norway when it was finished 225 years later. Nonetheless he gave them a kind greeting and asked, "Did you get a good education in France?"

"Time will tell," said Saemundur.

"You come at a good moment," the bishop said. "The church

at Oddi in Iceland needs a priest. You three, with your French schooling, are the best candidates."

The young men looked at one another.

"Which of us will you pick?" Saemundur asked.

The bishop frowned, gazing at them. Saemundur was tall and fair. As always, his expression was alert. Halfdan was dark and sturdy with a serious expression. Kalfur looked ordinary, but there was much to be said for ordinary people. An ordinary priest would not quarrel with his bishop.

The bishop thought awhile, then replied, "Whoever reaches Iceland and Oddi first will be the priest."

This was a contest worth winning. Oddi was a good church on a prosperous farm in the warm south of Iceland. They could do no better, unless they remained abroad, which none of them wished to do. The three Icelanders bid the bishop farewell and left his house.

Outside, Halfdan said, "I'm going to the docks to find a ship to Iceland."

"I'll go with you," Kalfur said.

Saemundur said nothing.

"I suspect you'll find a more unusual way to get home," Halfdan said. "And I won't be surprised if you arrive first. But I won't give up yet."

"Nor I," added Kalfur.

They said farewell to one another. Kalfur and Halfdan went toward the docks. Saemundur walked down to the harbor's stony shore. A cold wind blew, and snow fell heavily, dissolving into the gray waves. He climbed over rocks till he reached the water's edge. "Are you there?" he called to the devil.

A huge seal lifted its head from the water. "What do you want now?"

"My shadow, as always. More than that, I want a trip to Iceland. Can you take me there?"

"Of course," the seal replied. "But what do I get?"

"My soul, if you bring me to Oddi without a drop of water touching me. If you fail, I will get my shadow, which you have promised me more than once."

"I haven't done well, dealing with you," the seal said. "But I will make one more effort. Climb on my back."

Saemundur did as he was told, settling comfortably on the broad back. Although the animal had just risen from the water, its fur was dry.

"Are you ready?" the seal asked.

"Yes," Saemundur answered.

Off the animal went, swimming on the surface of the water like a whale. Water splashed, and spray flew, but not a drop touched Saemundur. Magic, he thought. Well, what did he expect?

Of course the seal was magical and rapid as well. The mountains of Norway soon vanished from sight. The two of them were alone on the ocean. Saemundur felt no inclination to talk with the devil, who never had much useful to say. In any case, the seal was keeping its head low, using it as a prow to cut the water. How was he going to spend the journey? As he wondered this, he felt a weight in his purse. He put his hand into the purse, pulling out the book Hermes the angel had given him. Here was the answer to his question. He would read poetry while the seal swam to Iceland. He had missed it in the devil's school, where there had been none except rhyming spells, which served their purpose but were not well composed.

He opened the book and began to read. At first this was difficult. The sky was overcast, with no sun visible; and the book was small, its pages full from side to side with tiny writing.

As he read, the process became easier. The book was increasing in size, he realized. Margins appeared. The pages began to glow with a pale light, and the black words — much larger now — stood out sharply. The book's weight increased with its size, till his wrists began to ache and he was forced to rest the book on his knees.

Only a fool climbs on the devil's back with no idea how to get off. Saemundur had a plan ready before he reached the shore at Nidaros in Norway. Now, as he looked at Hermes' book, he began to have second thoughts. There was no question the book was magical. He could see magic shining off its pages and feel magic bubbling off its cover. The magic did not flicker and burn and sting like the devil's magic. Instead it shone as steadily as the full moon in a cloudless sky and bubbled like water rising from a mountain spring, cold and clear and clean.

Surely he could do something with this marvelous object. Surely it would be courteous to use it. Kings and bishops liked to see their gifts put to use. God and his angels ought to be the same. He turned the book in his hands, trying to understand its properties.

Solidity was one; it rested on his knees like a block of stone. Good craft was another. Everything about it — parchment and writing and cover — was well and carefully done. He had never seen better work, not in Iceland or in Norway or in the devil's school. Finally, and this seemed important to him, the book was plain: black words on white pages, with no illumination. The black leather cover had neither gold nor jewels. It was what it was.

But no idea of how to use it came to him. Well, he thought, the journey was not over. Maybe something would occur. He went back to reading, being careful to glance up often, looking for the first sign of Iceland. At length he reached psalm 148, two poems from the end of the Book of Psalms: "Praise the Lord from the earth, ye dragons, and all the deeps." As he finished the poem, he glanced up. His homeland lay on the horizon: a dark row of jagged mountains. Saemundur sighed and closed the book.

The seal swam steadily on, till it was in the shallow water close to shore. Waves broke around them now, and foam flew. But not a drop touched Saemundur. Was he going to have to use his original plan? As he wondered this, an idea finally came to him. He raised the book above his head. At the same moment, the seal reached land. Its chest ground into the sand like a ship's prow, and it lifted its head, opening its mouth to give a shout of triumph. Before it could make a sound, Saemundur brought his book down as hard as he could on the animal's skull.

The seal grunted and rolled onto its side, spilling Saemundur into the ice-cold water. He scrambled up and waded to shore, still holding the book, which he had managed to keep dry.

The seal shouted in anger. Saemundur looked back, meeting the animal's eyes, which blazed like fire. "You will never get your shadow. I will keep it forever."

"Better that than my soul," Saemundur replied.

"I'll have that also," the seal cried, then turned and swam away, vanishing among the breakers.

Saemundur gave a sigh of relief and thanked God. He was nineteen years old and safe at home in Iceland. Somewhere ahead of him lay the church and farm at Oddi, which would be his. He wrapped his arms around the psalm book, which was still large and would make a good first addition to his library, and started inland.

Saemundur became a famous man, establishing a library and school at Oddi. No spells were taught there. Instead he taught respect for poetry and learning, kindness toward the poor, and good manners toward everyone. A few people called him Saemundur the Shadowless, since he never got it back. But most called him Saemundur the Wise.

Both Kalfur and Halfdan found churches of their own, though not on farms as good as Oddi. Halfdan married his sweetheart Thordis and raised a large family of blond and hardy children. Kalfur married also. His wife was a quiet woman with a good dowry. Instead of children, they raised horses, and Kalfur became famous for his animals' quality and training. People called him the Riding Priest. Halfdan was called the Lucky or the Fat, since he put on weight as he aged, and everything he did seemed to prosper.

The three comrades remained friends. Most years they met at the Althing, Iceland's great annual meeting. As time passed, they began to enjoy reminiscing about their days at the Black School. Those days were safely distant now, and they were well settled in their home country. It was fine to look back and remember how brave and clever they had been.

Kalfur and Halfdan never saw the devil again, but he visited Saemundur, and they had further contests. The devil did not win. He never does against noble-hearted people, who know how to think problems through and seize advantage of the situation and, most of all, how to make and keep friends. •

THE PUFFIN HUNTER

THERE WAS A MAN named Harald Palsson, who was a farmer in the west of Iceland. He had a small farmstead on the coast and kept a few sheep and horses, more for company than anything else. His income came from eider ducks and puffins. In nesting season, he gathered down from the eider nests. This is the best down on Earth and sells at high prices. But the work has to be done by hand, gently and carefully, so as not to frighten the ducks, since the duck eggs are still in the nest. Most of his income came from the ducks, but he also gathered puffin eggs. This was difficult work; he had to climb down the cliffs where the puffins nested and pull the eggs out of their burrows, putting them in a basket. It would have been safer to have someone else along to help him, but Harald was a solitary man, with little use for other people; and he was strong and confident and used to climbing. Don't think he was a fool. He used a rope and safety line.

In addition, he gathered the puffins themselves. He did this in the Faeroe Island way, scooping the birds out of the air with a big net on a pole, just as a butterfly collector catches butterflies, although the frightened, struggling, shitting birds were not as attractive as butterflies. Harald wrung their necks quickly. The puffins went to fancy restaurants in Reykjavik, as did their eggs. The eiderdown went to a merchant, who sold it to people who made expensive pillows in Europe and America.

As I said, Harald was solitary. His wife Helga had left him years before, running off with the postal deliveryman. She took their two children with her, first to the neighboring town and then, after her romance with the postman ended, to Reykjavik. It was a place that Harald disliked. He went there to deliver eiderdown to the merchant or puffins and puffin eggs to the chefs at fancy restaurants. But he left as soon as he could, and he saw the children rarely.

His former wife took up with a rich banker and moved to England. The children went with her. Harald didn't argue with Helga about the move, but he looked grimmer than before. He cheered up a little after the Icelandic banks crashed, and Helga's new husband was denounced in the Icelandic parliament and had warrants issued for his arrest. The family stayed in England and fought extradition, since the man would go straight to jail if he set foot in Iceland.

"Serves them right," Harald said.

Sometimes he went to the nearest town and stayed at the bar till he was too drunk to drive home. Then he'd sleep in his pickup truck or in the house of a friend, if it was winter and cold. These friends were people he had known from childhood, but he was not close to them, except when he was drinking. Then he'd tell stories from the old sagas and from the famous folklore collection of Jon Arnason — Harald was a well-read man — and make up rude verses. His most sarcastic poems were about bankers and politicians, though he could make up nasty verses about all the rich and powerful. His friends admired him for his quick wit and gift for poetry, also for his learning. But they were wary of him. Although he joked and made up clever poems, he always seemed cold at heart.

He had been different as a child, they said when he wasn't around, lively and imaginative and good at learning. They had expected him to go to college at the university in Reykjavik and become a professor. He had gone to the university right enough, but did not finish. Instead he came home to help his father, who was injured when a difficult horse threw him. There were lots of sheep then, and the father was no longer able to take care of them.

Harald stayed on the farm after his parents died, though he sold most of the sheep and horses. After that, he made his living from birds. He met his wife on one of his visits to Reykjavik. No one knew why they had married, or why the woman agreed to live on the farm. She was pretty, and he could be interesting, but that didn't seem to be enough. It was surprising the marriage lasted as long as it did.

All this time, Harald grew more and more grim. Maybe it had been hard for him to come home and work on the farm. Maybe it had been hard to lose his wife and then his children, though he never said anything. Looking at his hard face and cold, blue eyes, his friends were not inclined to ask questions.

So his life went until the day he caught an unusually large puffin in his net.

"Don't wring my neck," the bird said. "I am actually an elf."

"That seems hardly likely," Harald replied.

"If you let me go, I will reward you."

Harald made an impatient noise, took the puffin from the net, and wrung its neck. The moment it was dead it vanished, leaving nothing in his hands. His dog was with him, a handsome creature named Bruni. "That was a mistake," the dog told Harald.

"You can talk as well?" Harald asked. "If you thought so, you should have spoken sooner. What's done is done. At least there is no evidence left. No one will know I have killed an elf, if that's what I have done."

Then he went back to netting puffins. None of the rest spoke to him, and the dog said nothing more.

He went home finally, cleaned the birds, and put them in his refrigerator, planning to take them to Reykjavik the next day. He fed his animals and made dinner for himself, sat down, and ate alone, with not even the dog for company. Then he watched television till he was sleepy.

In the middle of the night a noise woke him. There was something in the house, making a flapping and crashing sound. With all his faults, Harald was not a fearful man. He got up and went out to the living room. A puffin was there, flying back and forth. There wasn't enough room for it to turn properly, so it crashed into the wall, then dropped to the floor and sat for a while, looking dazed and frightened. Then it took off again.

Harald watched briefly, then went to the front door and opened it. "Get out of here," he said, and waved his hand.

The puffin landed on the coffee table, sliding on the smooth surface, came to a stop, and stood up. It was definitely larger than the average puffin and had an unusually brightly colored beak. "I can't leave. I'm haunting you, and I have to do it in this form, because I was in this form when you killed me."

"I don't believe in ghosts," Harald said. "Especially ghosts that are puffins. Never, in all the folklore I have read, was there such a thing. Also, if I am remembering correctly, elves don't have souls and therefore can't become ghosts, any more than trolls can. They simply turn to stone and bother no one after that."

"That's trolls and not elves. We live longer than men, but die just like them; and we can become ghosts, though usually we don't."

Harald shut the door, since a cold wind was blowing in. It came out of the mountains and smelled of grass and ice, and it made him shiver. "I know that elves can become invisible. But I never knew that elves could become puffins," he said. "It's hardly a fair thing to do. Now, through no fault of my own, I have killed you."

"No fault!" the puffin cried. "I told you I was an elf. Why didn't you stop and think about that?"

"I don't believe in talking birds," Harald said.

The puffin made a sound of contempt. "In any case, you are stuck with me, and I am stuck being a puffin, which I don't expect to enjoy." Then the puffin dropped excrement on the coffee table. It seemed to be real excrement.

"Are you going to fill my house with bird shit?" Harald asked.

"I don't know," the puffin replied. "I've never been a ghost before."

Harald decided to go back to bed. "Could you stay in one place and not flap around? It bothers me. And try to shit in one place. It will be easier to clean up."

This time of year the sky remained light all through the night, though the sun went below the horizon briefly. But Harald liked dark when he slept and had good curtains. He lay in the dark, thinking about the ghost. He ought to consult a medium or someone at the Icelandic Elf School. But they would find out that he had killed the puffin. Was it a crime to kill an elf? He didn't think so, but it would certainly end up in the newspapers and online. All kinds of idiots would come to his farm and bother him. Not to mention the eider ducks, which were his main source of income. They weren't nesting at the moment, fortunately. But they might decide to find a new nesting site, if enough idiots trampled around and took photos and talked about ghosts in carrying voices.

What was he going to do? Maybe the ghost would disappear. Or maybe he could get used to it. It wasn't as bad as the ghosts in old stories, who threw sheep around and beat people. Glam in the *Grettis saga* was one such, until Grettir cut off his head and burned him. There were other, more recent ghosts, who were as bad as Glam. The Dark Deacon in the famous story tried to drag his fiancée into the grave with him; and there was a present-day ghost between Reykjavik and Keflavik, who waved at drivers, trying to distract them so they'd go off the road and crash.

Not that he believed in any of this; and a puffin could not do much harm.

At length he went to sleep. In the morning, the ghost was nowhere to be seen, though there was a pile of bird shit on the coffee table. He cleaned it off. There was a mark that wouldn't come out. Nonetheless, he sighed in relief.

Bruni the dog was outside the door. He said nothing, but got up and followed after Harald. The horses and sheep were cropping grass in the home field. They were silent as well. Maybe life would become ordinary again. No talking birds. No talking animals. He cared for the horses and sheep, then took the puffins he had killed to a chef in Reykjavik.

The drive back was difficult, through heavy rain. By the time he got home, he was tired. He made a sandwich and opened a bottle of brennuvin, then dozed in front of the television. There was a documentary on. Some fool was droning on about folklore. The elves who lived in rocks in Iceland. The trolls who had become rocks. He woke when the man began to talk about shape-changers, such as the Iceland settler Kveldulf, the grandfather of Egil Skallagrimsson, the famous poet and Viking. What was interesting about such people, the man said, was that they did not actually turn into an animal, as the werewolves in European folklore and American fiction did. Instead they sent their spirit out in the form of an animal while they slept at home. When Kveldulf dozed by the fire in the evening, his spirit became a huge wolf and roamed the countryside.

Harald grunted, turned the television off, and went to bed.

In the middle of the night, he woke to flapping and went out to the living room, turning on all the house's lights as he went. The puffin was back, flying around the room, hitting the walls and shitting.

"Stop that!" Harald shouted.

The puffin kept flying. Harald reached out and grabbed it from the air. For a moment, it was in his hands, warm and solid. He could even feel the hurried beat of its heart. Then it vanished.

"Don't do that," a voice said.

He looked around. The puffin was atop a lamp, looking precarious and dripping guano down the shade.

"I can't have you doing this," Harald said. "I won't get a decent night's sleep, and I'll be cleaning shit up every morning."

"You shouldn't have killed me," the bird said. "Elves make dangerous enemies."

Harald got the brennuvin and poured himself a stiff shot, then sat down on a chair that was not splattered with guano. "You vanished when I wrung your neck and vanished again when I caught you. That suggests that your body wasn't really present. Maybe it's still at home sleeping."

"Then why am I here as a ghost?"

"How can I tell? I think you should go back to your home, wherever it may be, and see if your body is there. If it is, tell your kin to wake you. That should end your problem and mine."

"I will think about it," the puffin said.

"Do that. In the meantime, stay in one place. You are making a mess of my living room."

Harald finished the brennuvin and went back to bed.

The next morning, the puffin was once again gone. Harald cleaned the living room and went out to care for the animals. Bruni the dog greeted him with a wagging tail, then said, "It isn't going to work."

"Why not?" asked Harald.

"I don't know, but I have a premonition."

"A dog with a premonition!" Harald exclaimed.

"What's so unusual about that?" the dog asked. "Everyone knows that some old ewes are weather-wise and can sense approaching storms. I can sense trouble coming toward you."

"I have not been the best person I could be," Harald replied. "But I don't believe I deserve talking animals."

He spent the day around the house, drinking too much brennuvin and listening to the national radio. Floodwater was coming out from under the Vatnajokul glacier in southern Iceland. That most likely meant that the volcano under the glacier had begun to erupt. Problems everywhere! At least his part of Iceland was not especially geologically active.

That night he could not sleep, even though he'd had too much brennuvin. He lay in bed in a kind of daze, thinking about ghosts. All the worst old stories came back to him. Finally he heard the sound of flapping wings and went out to the living room. The puffin was there, of course.

"Well?" Harald asked.

"I tried. I can't leave your house."

There were ghosts that seemed fixed in specific locations, though others could move around. The Dark Deacon, for example, who was able to ride a good long distance — even crossing a river — to get his fiancée and bring her to his open grave. It was his luck, Harald thought, to get a ghost who could not leave his living room. "What do we do now?" he asked.

"I will tell you where I live, and you can go there and talk to my kin."

"You want me to go to your house and tell your relatives that you are haunting me, because I killed you. Does it occur to you that your family might get angry?"

"I can't think of anything else to do."

He had a hangover, but it seemed like a good idea to pour

another shot of brennuvin. As he drank it, the puffin said, "You have an outcropping on your land. There are rocks piled up around it. You humans believe that these were put there by men, while clearing a field. This is not true. Elves piled the rocks up to make the entrance to their land more secure. In the middle is a boulder, which has points that look like turrets or horns. That is our gate. Go there and stand in front and say, 'Alfrun, Alfrun, your daughter Alfdis needs your help.'"

"You are a woman?" Harald asked.

"At the moment, I am a female puffin."

And still dripping guano down his shade, Harald noticed.

"When the door opens, a woman will stand there, richer and lovelier than anyone you have ever seen. Tell her that you know what has happened to me, but say you will not tell her, unless she promises you protection.

"She will give it and ask you in, and then you must tell my story. With luck, my kin will know what to do then."

"This is risky," Harald objected.

"Don't go in, unless she promises you protection. You will be safe then."

Harald went back to bed, feeling doubtful.

In the morning, he put on rubber boots and walked into the wet, mucky fields. He knew where the outcropping was. He'd played around it as a child, usually alone. He had one sister, who was much older than he was, too old for playing; and children his age rarely came to the farm. He made up for loneliness with imagination, pretending to be Grettir the Strong or one of the heroes from the American comics that his sister brought back from her job at the U.S. base at Keflavik. Climbing over the heap of rocks, he became Spider-Man in New York City and mighty Thor in Asgard. Squelching through the wet grass, Harald grimaced at his childhood self. What a dreamer!

He reached the outcropping and the horned boulder. The

ocean was in back of him. In the distance rose mountains. The rocks in front of him were black and pitted, patched with gray-green lichen.

"Alfrun," he said loudly. "Alfrun. Your daughter Alfdis needs your help."

There was silence, except for the whistling cries of birds.

"Alfrun," he repeated in a louder voice. "Damn you. Come out. Your daughter Alfdis needs your help."

More silence. A cold wind swirled around him, and he shivered, in spite of his good wool sweater.

A door opened in the boulder below the two horns. A woman looked out. As the puffin had promised, she was lovelier than any woman Harald had seen before. Golden hair flowered over her shoulders. Her blue eyes were as bright as stars. She wore a green robe, belted with gold. Gold bracelets shone on her wrists. "I am Alfrun, the mother of Alfdis. What do you have to say?"

"I will tell you what's happened to Alfdis, but only if you offer me protection."

"Against what?"

"Whatever harm might befall me."

"I can't protect you against everything. What if there's an earthquake or a volcanic eruption? A quarter of the people in Iceland died the last time the volcanic rift Laki erupted."

"Then I want as much protection as you can manage. In return, I will tell you about Alfdis."

The woman frowned, giving Harald a considering look. Finally she nodded and opened the door wide.

Harald stepped inside and found himself at one end of a large hall. As far as he could tell, it was made entirely of wood. The pillars and rafters were thick and could not possibly have come from any tree in Iceland. Where had the elves gotten such trunks? Norway? Or did they come from the days when

Iceland's shores had been lined with driftwood, including entire trees?

Chandeliers hung from the ceiling, their many candles casting a bright light. A long table went down the middle of the hall, covered with plates of food: racks of lamb, whole salmon and cod, heaps of potatoes glistening with butter, bowls of skyr and cloudberries, great slabs of cheese. People sat at the table. Like Alfrun, they wore old-fashioned clothes. They ate silently, drinking red wine out of tall glass goblets.

The woman gestured. Harald followed her through the hall, past the silent diners, and into another room. This one was small and dark, lit by only a few candles. A woman lay on a bed, apparently asleep. Another woman sat next to her.

The sleeping woman was young and almost as lovely as Alfrun. The waking woman was about Harald's age, solid and healthy looking, with red cheeks, dark eyes, and short, dark hair. She did not wear the same kind of clothing as the other people. Instead she had on an anorak, blue jeans, and tall rubber boots. She glanced up at Harald and said, "You are human."

"Yes," Harald said.

"Who are you?"

"Harald Palsson, and this is my land."

"I am Gudrun Gisladottir and human like you." She stood and held out a hand. After a moment, Harald took it. The woman's grip was firm, and she had a forceful shake. "The elves called me in, since I am a folklorist at the university. They thought I might know what has happened to Alfdis."

"Where is your car, if you drove here from Reykjavik?" Harald asked suspiciously. He did not like other people on his land.

"I parked a distance away and walked in. The people in the nearest town told me that you would not be likely to let me on your farm."

"This has nothing to do with my daughter," Alfrun said.

"What do you know about her condition?"

Harald took a deep breath and told his story. When he came to the puffin's death, Alfrun drew in her own breath, making a hissing sound. Gudrun reached down and touched the sleeping woman's hand, as if reassuring herself that it was warm.

Then he told them about the ghost. "I thought it might be her spirit, which has somehow become separated from her body, rather than a true ghost. Though I don't understand all the guano. I told her to find her home and see if she could re-enter her body, but she is trapped in my living room."

"I promised you no harm, though I would willingly harm you now," Alfrun said.

"The important thing is, can we reunite Alfdis's spirit and her body," Gudrun said. "If she cannot come here, then we will take the body to her. The elves don't like to travel in daylight, and there is little darkness this time of year, but we'll go when the sun is below the horizon."

"You think this is a good idea?" Alfrun asked.

"I can think of nothing else," Gudrun replied.

"Well, you know more about folklore than we do."

"I'm not sure how much use my knowledge is. There is much here that's new to me. But we will do what we can, and I may be able to get a scholarly paper out of this."

"I don't want fools coming to my farm, looking for elves," Harald said in a warning tone.

"I won't give your name or the name of your farm," Gudrun assured him. "But I can't keep quiet about this. It's new and valuable information about folklore."

They stayed in the room. Harald found a second chair and sat down. Alfrun offered to bring food, but he refused, trying to sound polite. Taking food and drink from elves could be risky. Gudrun asked for a glass of wine and drank it with evident pleasure.

"Aren't you afraid?" Harald asked, after Alfrun left the room.

"What? That I will go outside and find a hundred years have passed? Hardly likely. Alfrun wants her daughter back, and the elves find me useful. I have studied them more thoroughly than they have studied themselves."

So they waited, till Alfrun came back and said it was time. Six tall, handsome elves, dressed all in green, brought a litter into the room and lifted Alfdis onto it. They carried her through the hall, which was dark now. Other elves joined them, men and women, bearing torches. Harald followed them out of the hall and into the green fields of his farm. The sun was gone from view, but a pale, intense light still filled the sky. It made the elves' torches look dim. He didn't know why they had the torches. Maybe for ceremonial purposes. Everyone was silent.

The procession wound through Harald's wet fields, Harald coming last with Gudrun. "How can this be folklore?" he asked. "Isn't it real?"

"Yes, but how many will think so? Only ten percent of Icelanders believe in elves; and almost no one believes in trolls, though they throw rocks around in earthquakes and eruptions. Nowadays people believe in magma and the Mid-Atlantic Ridge."

Harald considered this. He was far more comfortable believing in plate tectonics than in trolls. As for elves — it was hard to think they were real, even though they walked in front of him, their torches flickering dimly and streaming in the wind.

The elves reached Harald's house. Alfrun opened the door. The litter carriers brought Alfdis inside and laid her on the coffee table and then came back out. "Come in with me," Alfrun said to Harald and Gudrun.

They followed her inside. The rest of the elves stayed outside, still holding their useless torches.

The living room was splattered with puffin guano, and the bird flew back and forth desperately.

"Daughter!" cried Alfrun.

The bird kept flying back and forth, crashing against the walls.

"Daughter!" Alfrun repeated.

Gudrun said, "Calm down and listen to your mother."

The bird landed on the sleeping woman's chest and looked around with dark eyes.

"You have spoken before," Harald said. "Speak now!"

The puffin huddled down, looking frightened.

"Alfdis!" Gudrun said firmly. "Speak to your mother."

The puffin made a small growling noise, such as puffins make in their nesting burrows.

This was terrible, Harald thought. The elves would think he'd been lying and become his enemies. The puffin would stay in his living room forever.

Alfrun frowned and half turned, as if to go.

Then the puffin spoke. "Mother."

"Ah," said Alfrun, and the elves outside repeated her, "Ah."

"You are still alive, Alfdis," Alfrun said to the puffin. "Feel the rise and fall of your chest. Enter your body, Daughter."

For a moment the puffin stood quietly, looking down at the sleeping woman. Then it said, "I can't."

"Nonsense," said Gudrun. "You are still alive, therefore you can't be a ghost. This unpleasant farmer may deserve to be haunted, but that isn't your job. Stop pretending."

"I can't," the puffin repeated.

Harald felt suddenly angry. He stepped to the sleeping woman's body and put his hands around her neck. The woman's skin was warm. He could feel the beat of her carotid artery.

Next to him, the puffin flapped its wings, but did not fly

away. Alfrun moved slightly, as if intending to do something. But Gudrun lifted a hand.

"I strangled you before and can do it again," Harald said harshly. "If I do, you will be a real ghost with no choice in the matter. There are better things to do with your life than haunt me."

"I can't."

"At least try! Or you will lose this body and your life."

The puffin hunched down. Harald tightened his hands around the woman's neck, and she groaned. The groan sounded almost like the growling cry of a puffin.

The puffin vanished. The sleeping woman opened her eyes, which were bright blue. Harald let go and stepped away.

Alfdis sat up and rubbed her neck. "I have been dreaming," she said to her mother. "A terrible dream. I died and became the ghost of a puffin."

"I will explain this later," Alfrun said. "But in the future, think carefully before you change your shape."

"I like to fly," Alfdis said stubbornly. "I like the feeling of having a beak full of fish."

"We will talk about this at home." Then Alfrun turned to Harald. "I promised not to harm you, and I will keep that promise. But I will not forgive you for killing my daughter once and threatening to do it a second time."

"I thought it might be possible to frighten her back into her body. I did what I did, and it worked."

"That is not a good excuse. You are no elf friend. Don't expect to see us again."

Then the elves — all of them, Alfrun and Alfdis, the elves gathered outside — vanished. Harald was alone in his guano-splattered living room, except for Gudrun and the litter. It remained on the coffee table: two long, smooth pieces of wood with green cloth between them.

"An artifact," Gudrun said. "I'll take it with me when I go."

"You're welcome to it," Harald replied. "I need coffee."

They went into the kitchen. Harald made coffee, and they sat and drank in silence. Meeting elves was unsettling, Harald thought. It led a person to doubt what was real, though he did not plan to stay in this mood of uncertainty. Life was easier with firm convictions.

Finally, in order to have something to say, Harald asked Gudrun how the elves reached her at the university.

"They can't be seen unless they want to be. They come into Reykjavik regularly, hitching a ride on a truck or even in a car. They have visited me before. This time they asked me to come and offer my opinion, since I was a folklorist and had studied the old stories about elves. I had no idea what to do. Would you have killed her?"

"No. It's not a crime to wring a puffin's neck, though I don't think I will do it again. I can make a living with eiderdown, and maybe I will get more sheep. But it is a crime to wring a living woman's neck. I'm not a murderer. As I told Alfrun, I thought it might be possible to frighten Alfdis into making a decision."

"I thought that's what you were doing, though I took a risk by lifting my hand. If you had done real harm to Alfdis, her mother would not have forgiven me."

Harald shook his head. He was tired and a little hazy. "I still don't believe in elves or ghosts."

Gudrun laughed. "I don't think you need to. The elves are going to avoid you in the future. I suspect you will never see them again. I'm hoping Alfrun's anger doesn't extend to me. I'd like to come here again and talk with her. Will you permit me to?"

Harald nodded and drank some coffee. Gudrun began to ask questions about his life. She was good at questioning, which made sense, since a folklorist had to get information out of old farmers and farmwives, as well as mediums, who could be a cranky lot.

He told her about his children, trapped in luxury in England, unable to come home to Iceland; and he told her about his sister, who had married an American and gone to live in a small town in Michigan, where her husband was a contractor. They had never been close, since she was so much older than Harald, and he hadn't seen her since she left. There were two nieces he had never seen, full grown now.

"Though I treasured the comic books my sister got for me. They're still around here somewhere in a box."

"That is American folklore," Gudrun said. "And not of interest to me. You aren't as unpleasant as I was told, though the trick you played on Alfdis was brutal. Maybe you are simply lonely."

"That might be," Harald said, "though I prefer to think I'm self-reliant."

She talked about herself a little while Harald made another pot of coffee. She was forty and single. A bad marriage had ended without children. It was something she didn't think about much these days. Better to let go of the past, which was something that ghosts did not do. In a sense, they did not realize that they were dead, just as Alfdis had not realized that she was still alive. "If you are dead, lie down and be quiet. If you are alive, live," Gudrun said.

"That sounds like good advice," Harald commented.

She liked her work and her apartment. She had been wise enough — or lucky enough — to not buy a house during the real estate boom. The apartment was expensive, but she didn't have a mortgage on a house that had lost half its value. She didn't like debt.

Harald nodded in approval.

At last Gudrun said she had to go. Harald rolled up the litter and put it in his pickup truck, then gave her a ride to her car. The sun was rising, and the sky — already bright — was becoming brighter.

He stopped by her car, a little Japanese thing. Gudrun got out of the truck and gathered up the litter. "I'm not sure how interesting this thing will prove. But I've never had an elf artifact before. If nothing else, I can hang it on a wall and remember the story of the puffin hunter.

"I'll come again with your permission, and maybe we can talk more. A man who can trick an elf is worth knowing, and so is a man who knows that there is more to life than haunting or being haunted."

"You can come," said Harald. "But I don't want you to think of me as something out of folklore. The man who tricked an elf! I am a plain farmer, who wanted the use of his living room."

"Good enough," said Gudrun. She drove off, one end of the litter sticking out a window. Harald watched till her car was gone from sight. Then he drove home. Bruni was waiting for him. "This looks promising," the dog said.

"You can still talk," Harald replied.

"Yes, and I can still have premonitions. I like that woman, and I think we will be seeing more of her."

"I was hoping that all the magic had left with the elves, and I was going to have a peaceful life without uncanny events."

"Well, you are mostly right," Bruni said. "I don't plan on talking much."

"Good," said Harald, and went to do chores. High up in the sunlit sky a dot was soaring. A white-tailed eagle, solid and real and beautiful. All at once, Harald felt unusually happy. •

MY HUSBAND STEIN

I ♦

THERE WAS A WOMAN named Signy, who was a journalist in Reykjavik. Her favorite work was writing about the environment, but she also did articles about art and fine dining. One does what one has to do in order to get by. In her spare time, she was working on a magic realist novel about Iceland in the twentieth century. She had read all the great Latin American writers, the Icelandic family sagas, and the novels of Halldor Laxness. But she hadn't found an approach to the novel which satisfied her.

She had a summerhouse in the East Fjords. This is a desolate area. The young people leave because there is no longer any work. The fishing villages along the coast are empty or mostly empty, and there are abandoned farms in the mountains. Signy didn't mind this. She liked solitude and the landscape; and the house had been cheap, because most people wanted vacation homes closer to the capital.

Every chance she got, she drove to her house, taking Highway One into the East Fjords and then an unpaved road up to the house. It stood on a high slope. Behind it was a cliff of black stone, and in front was a long expanse of uncut grass that ended suddenly in a drop-off. Beyond the drop-off was a headland, an island, and the glimmering ocean. It seemed she ought to be able to see all the way to Norway.

Although it was isolated, the house had all the comforts Signy wanted: a generator, a well, an inside bathroom, a living room furnished with comfortable furniture, and a tiny bed-room with a bed and a down coverlet. She spent most week-ends there and often entire weeks.

She especially enjoyed getting up in the morning, making coffee, and going out her front door to look at the ocean while she drank the piping-hot coffee.

One morning when she did this, she found a wild swan on the ground in front of her door. It was dead, its neck broken. She looked at it for some time and then called the police.

"That's strange," the voice on her cell phone said. "We have someone who lives not too far from you. We'll ask him to stop by."

She left the swan where it was and went inside. But she couldn't work on her novel. As the voice on the phone had said, the incident was strange and not in a way she liked.

Early in the afternoon a police car climbed the road to her summerhouse. It stopped. A big man got out and introduced himself. His name was Hrafn, which means Raven; but there was nothing ravenlike about him. His hair was blond, and his eyes pale blue. He looked solid and not especially clever.

He examined the dead swan. "I can't find any tooth marks, which means it wasn't a fox or a dog. In any case, I don't think a fox could kill a bird this big. In my opinion, a human stran-gled it and left it for you. Can you think of any reason why?"

"No."

"What are your relations with your neighbors?"

"I don't have any."

The policeman looked around. "That's true. Have you quar-reled with anyone in Iceland?"

"Only my mother and my ex-boyfriend."

"This does not look like something a mother would do," Hrafn said, and asked questions about her boyfriend, writing down her answers. When he was finished taking notes, he said, "I suspect this was done by a boy or several boys. As a rule, anything that looks strange and stupid has been done by boys or drunks; and this is a long way for a drunk to come in order to cause trouble. But I'll find out what your former boyfriend has been doing recently. You might consider going back to Reykjavik for a while. This place is lonely."

Signy shook her head. "I like it here."

"Then keep your door locked and make sure your cell phone is always close at hand. What are you going to do with the swan?"

"Bury it," said Signy.

"It looks fresh, and I know a butcher who will clean it. Can I have it?"

"With gladness," Signy replied.

Hrafn took the dead swan and left. Nothing more happened for a week and more. Signy got back to work on her novel, though she still wasn't satisfied with it.

One morning, ten days after she found the swan, she stepped out of her summerhouse and found a cod on the ground. It was as long as her arm. Its skin was copper, and so was the one eye she could see. The one visible gill moved slightly. It had not finished dying.

This was beginning to unnerve her. It was just after sunrise. No one was in sight, and this odd gift lay in front of her. Why? Was it a threat? If so, what did it threaten? If it was a gift, why was it left so strangely?

She called the police, then put the cod into her refrigerator. She had to take out both shelves and bend the cod to make it fit.

Midway through the afternoon, a police car drove up, and Hrafn climbed out. She showed him the cod.

"This still might be stupid boys, though how did they get here? You saw no one and heard no cars?"

"That's right."

He left her, walking a ways down the road, then back. "There are no hoof marks and no fresh tire tracks, though it rained yesterday. Of course, the boys might have come over the grass. But from where?" He glanced around at the empty countryside. "Your boyfriend is in Scotland, by the way. Are you sure you don't want to go back to Reykjavik?"

"I need to talk with editors," Signy said. "I will go back."

"A good idea," Hrafn said. "Are you intending to eat the cod?"

She took it out of the refrigerator and gave it to the big man. He thanked her and said, "The swan was delicious."

She drove back to her apartment in Reykjavik and spent three weeks there, missing her summerhouse every day. The city was too busy and noisy. She couldn't concentrate on her novel. Finally, she packed her car.

It was getting toward fall, and the days were getting shorter. But the air was mild and fresh once she got out of the city, and the drive to the lonely East Fjords was pleasant. The ocean was on her right. On her left mountains rose. Iceland's glaciers were shrinking, like glaciers all over the world. But there was still snow and ice on the mountains, and it shone in the morning sunlight. The ocean, when she could see it, flashed with white flecks of foam.

She reached the house, unlocked it, and put her groceries away, then set her laptop on the table in the living room. Beyond the front windows was the long slope of grass, the drop-off, and the shining ocean. She knew there was a novel in her, a good one.

Three days later, she found a heap of plants in front of her door, wildflowers which had been torn up by their roots. Many of the stalks were broken. Whoever had gathered them was either careless or clumsy.

She called the police again.

"This is getting to be a habit," said the voice on the phone. "I'll tell Hrafn about this. He likes mysteries."

Once again the police car climbed up the mountain, and Hrafn got out. He looked at the heap of flowers, which were all wilted now. "Someone likes you," he said finally. "Maybe it's a very strange schoolboy crush, but there don't seem to be any strange schoolboys around here. I've been asking. You have been private and kept your distance from everyone in the district. People around here don't know you. Usually you need to meet people or at least see them, in order to develop a fixation. So I have no suspects. I think you should consider selling the house."

By this time Signy was getting angry, and the flowers seemed less scary than the dead bird or the dying fish. Terrible things rarely happened in Iceland. She shook her head. She would not leave the house.

Hrafn didn't ask for the flowers. She took them to the drop-off and threw them into space, frightening some puffins, which flew off like rockets. That night she went to bed late, after making sure all the doors and windows were locked.

In the middle of the night, a voice woke her. "Signy," it called, deep and gruff. "Pretty Signy, you have refused all my gifts. Nonetheless I love you."

She got up and crept to a window, lifting the curtain just a little. There was a half moon in the sky. By its light she saw a grotesque figure on the grass in front of her house. It was tall and awkward looking, with a big head and long nose. Its hair was a great, stiff thatch, like a patch of dry weeds. It wore ragged pants and nothing else, and its bare feet were huge. Of course Signy knew what it was. Every Icelander learned about such creatures. It was a troll, though she had always thought that trolls were imaginary.

"I live in the cliff behind your house," the troll said. "And I have watched you since you moved in. Bit by bit, I have fallen in love with you; and I want to make you my wife, though I can't seem to find the right courting gifts. Believe me, I can make you happy. Do you see how big and thick my nose is? Well, my penis is even bigger and thicker. Imagine how it would feel! Imagine the pleasure I can give you!"

It would split her in two, thought Signy. "I need some time to think about your offer," she said.

"I'm running out of patience," the troll said. "And my penis is so eager to meet you that it frequently hurts. But I will give you a few more days. Decide quickly, pretty Signy." He stumped off on his huge feet and soon was out of sight.

Signy stayed awake for the rest of the night, thinking. She could go back to Reykjavik. She ought to be safe there. So far as she had ever heard, trolls never came into the city. But if they were real, as they seemed to be, then they were likely to be everywhere in Iceland, except the city. She could get another summerhouse, in another district, though she'd lose money selling this one. But the troll might show up at the new house. If she remembered correctly, they could travel fast and far.

Did she want to spend the rest of her life in Reykjavik? Or outside Iceland? As far as she knew, Canada did not have trolls, but she didn't want to live there; and the U.S. was out of the question.

No, thought Signy. She did not want to give up without a fight. But how was she going to fight? The police were not likely to be any help. She tried to imagine telling Hrafn that her stalker was a creature out of myth. The policeman did not seem like a person with a strong imagination.

She knew trolls turned to stone if sunlight touched them; and there were many rocks around Iceland that had once been trolls, or so tradition said. A clever woman would find a way to trick the troll into staying out after sunrise. But she couldn't think of anything, and a trick would be risky. She was pretty certain that he'd be able to crush her house with those huge hands and feet. She'd be left broken in the rubble or pulled out and torn to pieces. Trolls were dangerous.

So what was she going to do? Flee? Or take a risk?

She kept thinking until she had an idea. In the morning, she drove to Reykjavik and went shopping. Two days later, she returned to the summerhouse. She checked the generator and did some simple wiring. Then she ate dinner, turned out the lights, and waited for the troll.

Around midnight, she heard his voice. "Signy, pretty Signy. I have come for your decision. Will you marry me and meet my penis?"

"Just a minute," Signy replied. "I need to turn on some lights and get a good look at you. I won't marry someone I have never seen properly."

"Don't think the lights will do anything to me," said the troll in a warning tone. "I am immune to moonlight, starlight, firelight, and electric light. Only sunlight can do me harm."

The troll was suspicious. Signy hoped her plan would work. "I know that most kinds of light won't hurt you, and I want to take a good look at you, before I make a decision."

"Oh, very well," grumbled the troll. "But give me time to comb my hair."

Then she heard grunts and moans as he dragged a comb through his weedy hair. Finally he said, "I'm ready."

Signy turned on the new lights she had installed along the front of her house. They were the biggest full-spectrum lamps she could find, and they blazed down on the troll, casting a light that was almost like sunlight.

The troll shouted in anger or pain, Signy could not tell which, and then began to turn, as if intending to run away.

But he could not run. The light was not true sunlight, so it did not turn him to stone, as she had hoped it would. Instead it hardened his exterior. He became like lava that had cooled and formed a crust. Inside, the lava was still molten, but the crust constrained it.

The troll's limbs were most affected. They seemed frozen, one hand cast up, both feet planted wide. His torso was still capable of motion. It twisted slowly — oh so slowly — away from the light. His cry of pain or anger became a low, rumbling groan, so deep that she could barely hear it. Something must be happening to his mouth and throat.

After a while she made coffee and sat at the window, watching the troll. He kept turning, though with increasing slowness, until the sun came up. Then, as its long, level beams touched him, he turned entirely to stone.

That is that, thought Signy.

But it wasn't.

II ◆

Things were quiet for several weeks, and Signy got back to her novel. Then one night, when the moon was full, she heard groaning and sobbing outside. A harsh voice cried, "Oh, my husband Stein."

Signy looked out. There was another troll in her front yard, petting and stroking the boulder that had been the first troll. "What will I do without you, Husband?" the troll wife cried. "What will happen to our children? How can I care for them and feed them, without your help?"

Then there was more sobbing and petting.

The lights were still up on the front of her house. Signy knew she had protection if she needed it. "Let me tell you about your husband," she called.

The troll wife turned and stared at the house. She was big and gawky, with a head that looked too large for her body, and a long nose that looked too large for her head. Like the male troll, she was dressed in ragged clothing. In her case, it was a shift with many holes. "What about my husband?" she asked in a threatening tone.

Signy told her about the troll's courtship. When she was done, the troll wife kicked the boulder. "Sneaking around on me again, were you? You and your penis and your bragging. It was no bigger than my little finger and gave me small pleasure over the years. I suppose you thought a human would be easier to please, since every part of them is undersized.

"You gave her food that you could have brought home to your family! We would have enjoyed that swan! That cod would have made a fine dinner! You never gave me flowers, after all the years I worked my hands to the bone for you and your children!" She kicked the boulder again, this time harder, then hopped around on one foot, saying, "Ow!"

Finally the troll wife calmed down and introduced herself. Her name was Hrauna. She did not live in the cliff behind Signy's house, but farther back in the mountains; and she had two children, one a girl and one a boy. She was obviously a bit emotional, but she did have a problem. How was she going to care for her children without help from her husband Stein?

Signy thought about this. Her husband's transformation was mostly his fault, but she had to bear some responsibility. She could have moved to Reykjavik or Manitoba. Instead she chose to stay and fight. It could be said that she had killed the troll, in spite of her respect for ecology and the flora and fauna of Iceland.

"I can bring extra food out from the city, the next time I come," she told Hrauna.

"Thank you," the troll wife said.

Signy went to the city a few days later and came back with food, though she felt surprised about helping a troll. How could a modern woman be dealing with imaginary creatures from the past, who did not have good reputations? She might get in trouble. But the troll wife was already in trouble; and women ought to stick together, even if they were not the same species.

She put the food in a basket on her doorstep: bread and milk, cheese, smoked fish, fresh vegetables. Then she went inside, putting a chair by the light switch. After dark, the troll wife came, lit by a half moon. She must have been watching the house from somewhere close by in the mountains. She pawed though the basket and tasted the food, exclaiming. Everything was fine, except the vegetables. She wasn't familiar with cucumbers or with tomatoes, and they seemed strange to her, without much substance or taste.

"They will be good for your children," Signy told her.

"Well, then. I will give them a try. Thank you for your help, Signy. I will bring the basket back in three days." She left, carrying the basket off into the night.

After that they fell into habits. Signy brought extra food to her summerhouse, and Hrauna came down from the mountains with her two gray, long-nosed children. At first Signy stayed inside by the light switch. But gradually she came to trust the troll wife, and opened her door, setting her chair in the doorway.

Usually the troll wife came on moonlit nights. If she came on a dark night, Signy made sure all the inside lights were on. Bright illumination spilled out through the windows and the open door. She could watch the children tumbling in the grass and talk to Hrauna.

Bit by bit, she learned about the troll wife's life. It seemed hard to Signy, without any of the modern conveniences and imported luxuries that human Icelanders enjoyed. For the most part, Hrauna said, the trolls lived by fishing and hunting birds. Sometimes they took a reindeer or a few sheep, but they did this carefully, since they did not want to attract attention. Humans frightened them, with their machines that moved so quickly and made so much noise.

They spun and wove wool, taken from the sheep they took. But they were always short of cloth, and their clothing was always ragged and patched. Of course, they had almost no wood, since there was almost no wood in Iceland; and they lacked metal, except for the human tools they sometimes found.

"A hard life," Hrauna often said. "But it could be worse. There are far fewer humans living in the country these days, especially here in the east; and that is good. But those who remain are so noisy and disruptive!"

At the end of every visit, Hrauna would give the boulder a big, smacking kiss and then a kick. Off the trolls would go, carrying their food, into the darkness.

Maybe she would write a story about trolls for children, Signy thought. The novel didn't seem to be getting anywhere at the moment.

After this had gone on for several months, a police car came up the mountain, and Hrafn climbed out. "Have you had any more trouble?" he asked.

"No, though I put these lights up, just in case." Signy waved at the lamps on the front of her house.

Hrafn looked at them closely. Then he said, "I have a cousin who works in a market in the city. According to him, you are buying a lot of food these days. Why? You live alone."

"That's my business," said Signy. "It's nothing illegal."

"Lots of milk," said Hrafn. "I checked around. There are no children missing. Are you feeding a reindeer calf? Are you bribing your stalker with skyr?"

"No," said Signy. "As far as I can tell, he's gone."

"Ah," said Hrafn and looked at the lamps a second time. Then he wished her a good day, climbed into his car, and drove away.

His curiosity was worrying. But he had other things to occupy him, as Signy knew. The Karahnjukar hydroelectric project was nearing completion, and a flood of environmental protesters were coming into the East Fjords from all over Iceland and Europe. Signy had written about the project, since it and the protesters were big news; but she tried to avoid thinking about it when she was in her summerhouse. It wasn't the Iceland she wanted to see when she was in the East Fjords; it interfered with her novel, which was going to be modest and down-to-earth.

Everything about the project was oversized. Engineers had built the tallest dam in Europe on a bare highland at the edge of the Vatnajokul glacier; and the backed-up water from two glacial rivers had formed a huge new lake. That part was done, though the lake was still filling. Now giant tunnels were being driven through the rock to carry the water to an underground power plant. When the tunnels were complete, and the power plant was in operation, power lines — kilometers of them, strung on a forest of pylons — would carry electricity to the coast, over farms and farmers and flocks of sheep.

The local people mostly liked the project, since it brought money in, and they hoped their children would get jobs in the new aluminum plant in Reydarfjord and stay in the East Fjords.

It made environmentalists crazy. A pristine environment was being ripped apart, land flooded and rivers drained, and for what? Aluminum and four hundred jobs. What were Icelanders thinking of? Were they out of their minds?

Whether the answer was yes or no, the demonstrations meant that Hrafn was not likely to visit her house, which was south of all the action; and he wouldn't have time to worry about her grocery purchases, while angry demonstrators were pouring buckets of skyr dyed green over public officials.

She told Hrauna about the project one evening, while they sat by the door and the troll children played tag in the dark. The troll wife listened with interest. "That's what all the racket has been. We weren't happy when the Jokulsa i Fljotdal River dried up, and the Jokulsa a Bru River as well; and we don't care for the new lake in the highlands. We have been hoping that all the racket would end, and things would go back to the way they had been. But you are saying that still more is planned."

"Karahnjukar isn't finished, and there are plans for more dams and more projects. All Iceland has, besides fish and sheep, is energy; and it's a kind of energy that can't be exported, unless it's turned into something. So the government dreams of aluminum plants. We will grow rich by providing all the cooking pans that Europe needs."

Hrauna didn't understand this part. Trolls don't think much about energy. But she did understand the noise and the dry rivers and the lake where no lake had ever been. "You humans are as active as volcanoes, and it looks as if you are going to do as much harm. I think I need to tell our queen about this."

"Trolls have a queen?" asked Signy.

Hrauna looked embarrassed. "It's something that came from Norway. Lots of us say we ought to have a republic, as you humans do. This is a new land. We shouldn't keep the old ways. But we are slow to change.

"She isn't the queen of all the trolls in Iceland. Every region has its own king or queen. But here in the east, the one who rules is Hella."

Hrauna gathered up her children and left with a loping stride that looked awkward but covered ground rapidly. In a moment or so, she was gone from sight.

What will come of this? Signy wondered. Was it possible

that the trolls could stop the project? There were plenty of stories in Iceland about construction projects that ran into trouble when they tried to excavate areas where elves lived. The elves and their houses were not visible to most people. But all at once, equipment didn't work, and drills broke; nothing went forward. After a while, people would decide the problem was elves. Sometimes an elf speaker was called in to ask the elves if they would please move; and sometimes the elves would agree, provided they were given some peace and quiet while they packed up. Once they were gone, the project had no further trouble. In other cases, the elves stayed put, and the project went around the elves. There were odd jogs in roads in Iceland, due to elf towns.

She had never heard of trolls interfering with construction, but then she had never given trolls a lot of attention. First of all, she had never believed they existed. Second, she had the impression that they kept to the mountains and the interior wastelands; but that was where the project was being built.

Two nights later the troll wife came back. She did not bring her children. "The queen wants to see you," she told Signy. "She wants to hear the story of these troubles from your own mouth. Will you come with me?"

"To what place?"

"Her great hall. It's back in the mountains, and there is no human road. But I can carry you."

At that point, Signy had to make a decision. It was frightening to think of going alone to a troll stronghold. But she was a journalist, and this would make a fine story.

"How do I know I will be safe?" she asked Hrauna.

"Bishop Gudmund took care of most of our troublemakers long ago. Those of us who remain are peaceful."

"Except your husband."

"Stein was a fool led by his penis; and — to be fair — he did not threaten you with anything except marriage."

"That seemed like a threat to me," Signy replied.

"He wasn't much as a husband," the troll wife admitted. "I give you my word that you will not be harmed, and the word of the troll queen as well."

If she didn't go, she would spend the rest of her life thinking of what she had missed. Signy nodded.

"Tomorrow night, then," Hrauna said. "I will come as soon as it's dark."

The next day Signy looked at her cell phones. She had a new Nokia with absolutely everything, but it was bulky and difficult to use. Instead she charged an older phone, which included a camera and GPS, but nothing else. She put spare batteries in her pocket and added a small audio recorder. No one would believe her, unless she had proof, which meant pictures and an audio recording.

She was too restless to sleep, and so she drank coffee and watched the ocean, gleaming blue at the end of her slope. Her grass was yellow now. A pair of gyrfalcons raced across the sky.

A little after sunset, Hrauna arrived. Signy closed her door and locked it, putting the key in her pocket. The troll wife gathered her up. Signy wasn't a large woman, but she was surprised at how easily the troll wife lifted her. "You are light," Hrauna said, and turned and set off at a loping run.

As awkward as the troll wife had always seemed, her gait felt smooth, like an Icelandic pony's tolt, a gait that no other horse had. Signy was not a rider, but she had been told that a person could sit on an Icelandic pony and drink tea from a china cup, while it tolted. If she had brought tea and a china cup, she could have done the same in Hrauna's arms.

In the dark, under the blazing stars, she had no idea of time. But Hrauna did not stop running soon. The mountain peaks were invisible, except as patches of darkness against the stars.

She felt the land, rather than saw it, as Hrauna loped up slopes, then down into valleys. After a while, Signy dozed.

She woke when Hrauna stopped. Opening her eyes, she looked around. The stars were gone. Fires shone in front of them. The troll wife set her down. They were inside a cave or tunnel. Lumpy figures holding torches stood a short distance away.

"Go forward," the troll wife said.

Signy walked farther into the tunnel. The figures were trolls. Like Hrauna, they were large and gray with rough skins, long noses, and large hands and feet. They wore torn shirts and ragged pants, tied at their waists with pieces of rope; and the torches they carried were made of twisted reeds.

She was looking at poverty, Signy thought, the kind of poverty no modern human Icelander knew. There were no flashlights here, no imported shirts and sweaters, no Chinese running shoes.

"Come," a troll said harshly, and turned. She followed him along the tunnel, which slanted down. Hrauna came behind her, as did the other torchbearers. Their long shadows stretched past Signy, moving on the tunnel's walls and floor. The air grew dry and dusty. Drawing it in, Signy tasted stone.

At last they arrived at a large, round cave. It must have held a pool of magma once. Now it was empty except for a high chair, roughly made of volcanic stone. More trolls with torches stood around the chair. In it sat a heap of lava, all lumps and crevices, with two eyes like obsidian chips.

The lava moved, leaning forward and fixing Signy with its obsidian eyes. A grating voice spoke.

> *"Harsh the hand of Signy,*
> *dealing doom to Stein.*
> *Helpless the troll,*

hopeless the ending,
when the battle-swan turned on the lights."

"Well, yes," said Signy. "But it was in self-defense."

The rock in the throne leaned back. It was a woman, Signy could see now, with long, pendulous breasts and broad thighs. The gray, pitted face was barely a face, though Signy could make out the eyes, a slash of a mouth, and the nose. A ragged shift covered the queen's torso. On her head was a crown made of gold and garnets. It looked ancient, like the art of the Viking era. The queen spoke again:

> *"Tell the tale of human vengeance,*
> *rock ripped and rivers emptied,*
> *fire-old Iceland cored*
> *like Idun's apples,*
> *giving nothing more to gods and men."*

Signy had studied the old stories while doing research for her book. She knew that Idun's apples kept the Norse gods from aging. But she didn't remember a story about the apples being cored.

Hrauna poked her. "Tell the story, and speak loudly, so everyone can hear."

Signy looked around. She had thought the cave was empty except for the queen and her retainers. It was not. Trolls stood along the walls, their gray bodies seeming to merge with — or emerge from — the stone. The smallest were knee high to her. The tallest towered ten meters or more. Like all the trolls she had met so far, they were dressed in ragged clothing: shifts, long shirts, and pants with torn bottoms. Their feet were bare and huge.

Hrauna poked her again, and Signy told the story of the

hydroelectric project. The trolls were as silent as stone. In front of her, the queen remained so still that Signy was no longer able to see the person, only a lump of lava with a crown perched on top. There were rocks this oddly shaped all over Iceland, though they did not usually have crowns.

She came to the end of the story and stopped. The troll queen finally stirred. "I will speak plainly and in prose," she said. "The old human heroes could make up poems in the most difficult of times, in the middle of battle and even while being cut down by their enemies. I am not them. Your kin are destroying my land, Signy."

"I have nothing to do with this," Signy protested. "I am opposed to the project and have written against it."

"I did not say you did," the queen replied. "I said it's being done by humans, who are your kin; and now we must decide what to do, if anything."

"Break the dam," said a harsh voice behind Signy.

A second troll said, "Fill in the tunnels."

"Let Jokulsa a Bru run free, as it has always done," a third added.

"What right do humans have to do this to us?" a fourth voice asked.

"Bishop Gudmund would not permit this," another harsh voice put in. "He knew even trolls need a place to live. That's why he left one part of the cliff at Drangey unblessed, so we could live there and get in and out."

This was another story Signy knew, though not from research. It was both famous and old. Bishop Gudmund the Good Arason had been dead for centuries.

The queen lifted a gray, pitted hand. "We will consult about this. Because you are a saga writer, Signy, I would like you to hear our decision. As Odin said in the *Havamal*, everything dies except fame. We want our story told."

The hand dropped. The queen slumped, until she looked like a lump of lava once again.

Hrauna tugged at Signy. "Come away."

She followed the troll wife into a new tunnel. Was this the time to take out her phone? She had forgotten it while in the throne room. But there was no light except the torchlight flickering behind them. If she tried to snap a picture, the flash would go off, almost certainly frightening Hrauna and the other trolls. Frightened folk were dangerous. She decided to wait.

The torchlight faded till they were in complete darkness. Hrauna took Signy's hand. Strange, to feel those huge, hard, rocklike fingers folded around her fingers. They walked a long way like this. She was in the heart of Iceland, Signy thought, the core the troll queen had mentioned in her poem. There was nothing here except dry air, the smell of rock, and their own footsteps, echoing between bare stone walls.

Hrauna said, "You will stay here."

"Where?"

"We are in a little room, made by a bubble in the lava. It's large enough for a human. I will bring you food and light. Sit down. Be comfortable."

Signy sat down. Hrauna stumped off. After a while, she opened her phone. Light shone out, which was comforting, but she could not find a connection. She took several pictures, using the flash. There was nothing except bare rock. Hardly interesting, or proof of anything. She put the phone away.

Hrauna came back finally, carrying a bowl and lamp, both roughly made from stone. The lamp burned oil, which had a familiar smell. The bowl was full of something pale gray and lumpy.

"What is this?" Signy asked.

"Skyr."

"Why is it gray?"

"We put in a little ground rock to give texture and flavor. Your human skyr is bland."

The troll wife gave her a bent pewter spoon. This was clearly human. Well, the East Fjords were full of empty farmhouses and fishing villages. If the trolls scavenged, who was harmed? She used the spoon to eat. The skyr was gritty, but edible. A little lava dust would do her no harm.

"The council will take a while," Hrauna said, and sat down. "We trolls do not decide quickly."

This was a good time for an interview, Signy thought, and to find the answers to some questions which had begun to occur to her. She reached into her pocket and turned on the recorder. "What is the oil in the lamp?"

Hrauna looked embarrassed. "Kerosene. We don't need much. For the most part, we like the dark. But what we need we steal from gas stations. We used to use the oil from seals and whales, but it's hard for us to fish in the ocean. Our own boats wore out long ago, and there aren't as many human boats to borrow as there used to be. We don't know how to operate the ones with engines. It's easier to steal the kerosene."

"If you like darkness, why do you use torches and lamps?"

"For you, at the moment," Hrauna answered. "And while we don't need light to see, we enjoy it. Moonlight and starlight are lovely, shining on the mountains and the ocean. Fire is useful for cooking, and there is something comforting about the light of torches and lamps. Only sunlight is dangerous."

Signy thought about this for a moment, then remembered another question. "The queen spoke about Idun's apples getting cored. I don't know that story. Is there one?"

"Yes," said Hrauna. "I will tell it, if you wish. It will take up time."

"Please do," Signy said.

The troll wife began, speaking formally, as if the story came from long ago, when people — even trolls, apparently — spoke in a more elevated fashion.

LOKI AND THE APPLE CORER

"The goddess Idun tended a grove of apple trees that blossomed and bore fruit at the same time. The blossoms were white, with an aroma that was both sweet and delicate. The apples were golden skinned, with crisp flesh as white as the apple blossoms and a sharp, almost bitter flavor. Everyone who ate them found them delicious. The gods ate them daily, and the apples kept them young.

"Now and then Idun became tired of tending the grove and took a vacation. She had a summerhouse in the mountains far from Asgard. Sometimes she went there alone, and sometimes the god Tyr went with her. He was the bravest of the gods, and she was the kindest of the goddesses. They got along well.

"While she was gone, one of the other goddesses tended the apple grove. Usually it was Frigga, who was Odin's wife, a woman both lovely and wise. But in this story, Freya the goddess of love was chosen.

"At first, everything went well. But then Freya became irritated by the apple cores. When the gods ate the apples, they chewed down to the cores. But the seeds were especially bitter, so they ate no farther. Instead they tossed the cores into the grass that grew beneath the apple trees.

"After a day or two, the ground under the trees absorbed the cores. Until then, they were slippery underfoot; and they attracted bugs, which Freya did not like. She was a fastidious goddess with a strong sense of her own beauty. She did not like the way she looked when she batted at flying bugs or slipped on apple cores. So she began to complain to the other gods about their bad manners and lack of neatness. Idun had never done this, and it was difficult for the gods to change their habits. Freya became more and more strident, and the gods no longer took pleasure in eating the apples.

"What should they do with the cores, if they did not throw them into the grass? No one wanted to walk around carrying an apple core as it turned brown, and it seemed wrong to toss the cores in a midden heap. They were, after all, magical and in Idun's care. She might ask about them when she came home. Finally, Loki said he had an idea.

"Loki was unreliable, and the gods should not have listened. But they were tired of Freya's complaints. They told Loki to try his idea. He left Asgard, going to the realm of the dwarves, who were the most skillful makers anywhere, and described the thing he wanted them to make.

"'We can do this,' the dwarves said. 'In return, we want the apple cores.'

"'Why?' asked Loki.

"'You gods remain forever young, but we dwarves age. We intend to plant the apple seeds and grow our own grove of youth.'

"Loki, who never thought things through, agreed. The dwarves made the device he wanted. It did not look exactly as he imagined. The dwarves improved the idea, as they usually did.

"It was a metal box with a hole on top. A cup rested on the hole, and the hole went through the cup. To the side was an arm on a hinge. A cylinder was attached to the middle of the arm. When the arm was pulled down, the cylinder cut through whatever rested in the cup; and the cutout piece dropped into the box. Then the arm could be lifted, and the object in the cup picked up: a perfectly cored apple.

"'This is excellent,' Loki said.

"'We have added some magic,' the dwarves said. 'The apples will always rest firmly in the cup, without moving or shifting position, and the cylinder will always cut cleanly. The cores will never get stuck in it, but will always drop neatly into the box. It seems like a lot of work to us, when a knife would work just as well. But we have done as you asked. We expect to get the apple cores in return.'

"'You will,' said Loki, and he took the device back to Asgard. It worked exactly as the dwarves had promised. Freya was no longer troubled by bugs or slippery footing. She returned to her usual lovely and pleasant self. The gods congratulated Loki and ate their apples in peace, enjoying the beauty of the apple grove and the sharp flavor of the fruit. Every day Loki took the full box away and returned with it empty.

"He did not take the cores to dwarves as he had promised, but to a hiding place only he knew. Maybe he had a plan for using them, or maybe he was simply refusing to keep his word. He was a liar by nature.

"One day soon after, the goddess Frigga looked in her mirror. A white hair shone like silver in her golden hair. She stormed to her husband Odin, saying, 'Something is wrong.'

"Odin looked at her keenly with his one sharp eye. 'You are right,' he said. 'I can see fine lines on your face, though I don't think they would be visible to anyone except me. I don't think this problem is with you alone. My missing eye has been paining me; and yesterday Thor complained to me about aches in his hammer hand.'

"'Something has happened to the apples,' said Frigga.

"'Yes,' said her mighty husband. He lifted the raven named Thought from his shoulder and told it, 'Fly to Idun, and tell her we need her in Asgard.'

"The raven flapped its wide, black wings and took off, sailing into the sky. Idun returned as soon as she got the message.

"'What have you done with the apple cores?' she asked. 'It is the bitter seeds that keep my trees young.'

"Everyone turned and looked at Loki.

"'He did it,' Freya said. 'He has the apple cores.'

"Tyr had returned with Idun. He had only one hand, but it was powerful. He grasped Loki around the neck and lifted him off the ground. 'I will hold you here until you strangle, unless you tell us what you have done with the apple cores.'

"Loki could not speak, but he waved his arms desperately, and Tyr set him down, shifting his grip to Loki's arm, so the trickster could not run away.

"'I put the cores in a glacier, so they would not decay. Let me go, and I will bring them to you.'

"'Nonsense,' said Tyr. 'You will lead me to your hiding place, while I keep a firm grip on you; and I will bring the apple cores back to Idun.'

"That is what happened. As soon as Tyr spilled the cores onto the ground below the apple trees, they vanished into the soft, green grass. In a day or two, they were completely gone, absorbed into the ground. The trees regained their power, and the gods became young again. But Tyr let go of Loki in order to gather up the cores, and Loki ran off laughing. He had kept some of the apple seeds and planned to do something with them, though he wasn't sure what. And that is the story."

The troll wife stood up. "I need to look after my children."

She left, and Signy lay in the bare stone room, the lamp flickering beside her. She had thought of herself as a modern woman, with her cell phone and computer, always connected to the World Wide Web, even in the lonely East Fjords. Now she was in this place out of myth, and she had a new myth about the ancient gods — one she knew she had never heard —

on her recorder. Nothing was modern, except her recorder.

She drifted into a dreamless sleep and woke when Hrauna shook her.

"We have made a decision. The queen wants you to hear it."

She got up. "Do you have a bathroom?"

"Pee here," said Hrauna. "We don't intend to use this room again."

She did, while Hrauna waited in the tunnel. Then they walked through darkness together, till torchlight appeared in front of them. Signy felt dirty, in need of a shower and tooth-brush. Maybe the trolls wouldn't notice her rumpled hair and morning breath.

Everything was as before: the torches, the trolls, the queen in her chair like a lump of lava. The garnets in her crown glinted redly.

> "Grim the choice
> that humans give us.
> Canyons call us.
> Rivers complain.
>
> "Hard the choice
> and hard the leaving,
> but leave we will
> our lovely land."

"Leave?" asked Signy, feeling disappointed. She had been hoping, she realized, that the trolls would interfere with the project.

"Yes," said the troll queen. "Elves have been able to stop human projects, though never anything this big. We have not. As much as possible, we avoid humans.

"We will move into the interior, either into one of the new

national parks or to land so bare that humans will never find a use for it."

"But there are plans for more projects," Signy protested.

"That is your problem. We will do what we must."

"Would you mind if I took a photograph of you?" Signy asked. "This is a historic moment."

The troll queen frowned, then nodded. Signy took out her camera and aimed it. The flash went off. The trolls shouted in surprise and fear. "It is not sunlight," Signy said reassuringly.

"Nonetheless, it is disturbing," the troll queen said. "Don't do it again. Now, go. Write this story down, so people will remember us and our decision and our loss."

Hrauna led Signy from the troll throne room and though the tunnel that led outside. It was night, and the sky was overcast. Signy could see nothing, though she thought she could feel the mountains around her: vast, invisible shapes. Hrauna gathered her up and carried her home through the darkness.

"We may not meet again," the troll wife said after she set Signy down. "Farewell."

Surprised at herself, Signy hugged the troll wife and wished her the best of luck.

The massive, lumpy creature hugged her in return, then left, loping into the night with her odd gait that looked clumsy but was rapid and smooth.

Signy went inside and turned on the lights. She checked the picture in her cell phone. Only the troll queen was visible, and the glare of the flash had removed all detail. Hella was an oddly shaped rock resting on another oddly shaped rock. The garnet crown was a handful of glints, which might well have been crystals in lava. Her two eyes were two more glints. Well, that was not useful, Signy thought. She turned on her recorder and listened to Hrauna's story. The troll wife's harsh voice was perfectly understandable, though she did not speak modern Icelandic. This was a voice from the past. She would take the recording to someone at the university, an expert on Old Icelandic, and see what response she got. But it was not proof that trolls existed, only that someone somewhere spoke an odd version of Icelandic.

The troll queen had asked her to write down the story of their meeting and the trolls' decision. She would do that. But she had no proof. As far as anyone could tell, the story was fiction. Fiction or not, it said something that was important, something that was true, whether or not people realized it was true.

And that is that, she thought.

But it wasn't.

III ◆

A week or two later, Hrafn drove back up. He climbed out of his car and said, "I forgot to mention, the cod was excellent. It may have been the best cod I have ever eaten. And it was so handsome that I took a picture of it, before I began to clean it. Thank you."

Signy told him he was welcome.

He looked at the lights on the front of her house again. "I have been thinking about your groceries. Have you been making skyr for the demonstrators? They are pouring it on all kinds of respectable officials. Someone is making it, a lot of it, and in every possible color."

"No," said Signy. "If you must know, I have been feeding the puffins."

"Milk and cookies?" Hrafn asked.

"I am eccentric."

"It might be interesting to eat a puffin that has been fed on milk and cookies," Hrafn said thoughtfully. "If you decide to cook any of your guests, give me a call."

He walked around the boulder that had been Stein. "I remember this from my last visit. It was new then."

"A gift from my stalker," Signy said. "His last gift, before he vanished."

"How did he move it?" Hrafn wondered.

"I can't tell you."

"There's a story here," Hrafn said. "If I had time, I would try to find it out. But I must defend respected officials from skyr."

He left and she went back to working on the story of the trolls. Another week passed. Then one night there was a knock on her front door. She opened it. Hrauna stood there, blinking at the bright electric light.

"Hrauna!" Signy said with pleasure.

"I have another message from our queen. We are leaving in ten nights, and she would like you to come as a witness. I could take you there, but I will not be able to bring you back. Can you get to the Dark Canyon in your noisy metal machine?"

"Yes," Signy said. There was a road, though she had not traveled it since the Jokulsa a Bru River stopped flowing through the canyon. She had gone to say farewell to the river, before the dam shut it off. A sad journey.

"Come in ten nights. There will be a moon, so you will be able to see. I will meet you at the canyon's edge. Don't worry about finding me. I will find you."

"I will come," said Signy.

Hrauna left, and Signy went back to reading. She was going back over all the myths about the old gods, looking for a version of the story of Loki and the apple corer. So far she had not found it.

The night came, and she drove to the Dark Canyon. The sky was clear, except for a few clouds in the east over the ocean. The moon was three-quarters full. She had no trouble along the way. When she reached the canyon, a lumpy figure stepped into the road and waved her down. It was Hrauna. "Stop your machine here," the troll wife said. "I will lead you the rest of the way."

They walked over rough ground to the canyon's edge. She could not estimate the depth, since most of the canyon was hidden by shadow. But she knew it varied between 100 and 150 meters deep. Before the project, a turbulent river had filled the bottom. Now all that remained was a much smaller stream. She heard wind whispering and no other sound. Moonlight lit the far wall, maybe seventy-five meters away. She could see the sheer, bare, dark rock clearly.

"Now what?" she asked.

"Wait," answered Hrauna.

She peered into the darkness. Clouds were blowing in, and the moonlight became less clear and steady. It moved over the canyon walls, growing dim, then bright, then dim again, as clouds flew past the moon.

"We hoped for this," said Hrauna. "We did not want people to see us leaving."

"But you picked a moonlit night."

"For you."

Now she saw motion in the moving light. Large figures were climbing up the canyon walls.

"The trolls," said Hrauna. "We had many settlements along the river. All are leaving."

The first figures reached the canyon rim, some on their side, though none close to them. Most were on the far side. They lowered ropes and pulled up packs. The packs were loaded on waiting trolls, who moved off, bent double by the weight of their loads.

More trolls arrived on the surface. Some were children, clinging to their mothers' backs. Others seemed ancient and were brought up in rope slings. They all gathered packs or bags and moved inland.

More came, then more. There were hundreds.

Now she saw other figures among the trolls. They were smaller and slimmer and moved with far more grace.

"Who are those?" she asked.

"Elves. They are leaving too. This project is too big for them to stop."

When they reached the surface, the elves seemed to flicker, becoming impossible to see in the changing moonlight. Was that a person or a shadow moving over the bare rock among the trolls?

Still more figures climbed up, among the trolls and elves. These seemed both insubstantial and faintly luminous. They gleamed in the Dark Canyon like wisps of moonlit mist.

"And those?" asked Signy.

"Human ghosts. We are taking their bones with us, so they won't be left alone here."

A man climbed onto the rim not far from them. He was dressed like someone from the saga era. A sword hung at his side. His hair was blond, and he had a short, neatly trimmed blond beard. He turned and bent down, helping a woman onto the rim. She also appeared to come from the early days of Iceland. Two gold broaches gleamed on her shoulders. Her hair was long and very blond, more like silver than gold.

They paused a moment, hand in hand, then looked at Signy and Hrauna. The man's eyes were pale and piercing. His gaze seemed to go through Signy like a spear. What did he see? How did she appear to someone so old and so obviously heroic? It was like looking at Gunnar of Hlidarend or Grettir Asmundarson, though neither of them had died around here.

The woman nodded graciously, like a queen. Then the two of them turned, and Signy saw a great, dark splotch across the back of the man's shirt. "What is that?" she asked.

"I don't know for certain," Hrauna said. "But I think it's blood from his death blow. He must have been struck from behind, maybe by someone he trusted."

The couple were moving away, heading inland. The woman looked unharmed, but she had died young.

"Who are they? What is their story?"

"Dead people from long ago," said Hrauna. "I don't know otherwise."

The departure continued: trolls and elves and ghosts. More clouds covered the sky. The moonlight became a dim, erratic glimmer, and Signy found it more and more difficult to see anything.

At last, Hrauna said, "I must go now. The queen wants you to describe this. It may not seem important to humans, but to us leaving a place where we have lived for so long matters."

"I will do it," Signy said.

Hrauna walked away along the canyon's rim, following the two ghosts.

Only a few figures still climbed the canyon's walls. Signy exhaled. She was not sure what she was feeling, but it was something profound.

"That was a sight," a voice said behind her.

She started. A hand grabbed her arm. "Careful, or you will fall in the canyon."

She turned. It was Hrafn, dressed in casual clothing, with binoculars around his neck.

"What are you doing here?"

"I followed you from your house with my lights out, then parked and crept as close as I dared. I didn't want to attract the troll's attention.

"I've been watching you when I have the time. Something was obviously going on. Either it had to do with the demonstrations, though I thought that was unlikely, or it had to do with trolls. That was the only reason I could imagine for the full-spectrum lights on the front of your house, and that was the only explanation I could think of for your new boulder."

He grinned, looking happy. "It's lucky that I was near when you drove out tonight. I would have hated to miss this."

"What are you going to do?" Signy asked.

"Nothing. It's not illegal to consort with trolls."

"They are leaving. We have driven them out with the project."

"I realize that." He glanced at the canyon. As far as Signy could tell, it was empty now. "I have read your articles. I know you don't like the project."

"Do you?"

"I haven't decided. It may prove to be too expensive. One of my cousins is an economist, and he worries about that. Iceland's economy is always fragile, Ingolf says, and we have to be careful how we spend our money. Another cousin is a geologist, and he isn't sure the land here is entirely stable. What happens if there are earthquakes or volcanic activity? Will the dams and tunnels hold?

"But I grew up here, and I always wanted to return. I was lucky enough to find the job I have. But most of the people I grew up with are in Reykjavik. If the project brings work here, that is good; and if it helps the national economy, that also is good. So I haven't made up my mind.

"Why don't you drive home? I'll follow with my lights on and make sure you are safe."

She could think of no argument. So she drove back to her summerhouse, the headlights of his car behind her.

After they had both stopped, he got out and walked to her car. "There's a new restaurant in Reydarfjord that isn't bad. One of my cousins is a partner."

"The one who works in the market?" Signy asked.

"No. The economist. He isn't sure Karahnjukar is a good idea, but he thinks it will keep his restaurant in business. Would you join me for dinner there sometime? I owe you at least one dinner in return for the swan and the cod."

He was far more clever than she had thought at first, and he was the only person certain to believe her when she talked about trolls. She wanted to know how he'd kept track of her. Had he simply been watching with binoculars, or was he using some kind of electronic device? She wanted to know the answer to that question; it might lead to an article. Are the Icelandic police like the FBI? Has 9/11 led to the erosion of Icelandic liberty?

It was also true that she found him attractive. If he didn't turn out to be a spy or criminal, like the police in America, she would like to get to know him better.

So she told him, "Yes."

He smiled and nodded, told her good night, and left.

She unlocked her door and went in, turning on the lights. Her little summerhouse looked strange and unfamiliar after the sight of the trolls leaving the Dark Canyon. Who was she? And what was this land that she had thought she knew? She would have to rethink her novel, though she wasn't sure she wanted to include trolls. The ghosts, maybe.

Signy made coffee and set out some cookies. The troll children wouldn't be coming back to ask for them. She would have to eat them herself.

Then she sat down and opened a notebook.

And that was that. ·

NOTES ON THE STORIES

Introduction

My main reference for the introduction was Gunnar Karlsson, *Iceland's 1,100 Years: History of a Marginal Society* (Reykjavik: Mal og Menning, 2000).

The quote on p. xi by Grimur Jonsson Thorkelin is from Kevin S. Kiernan, *The Thorkelin Transcripts of "Beowulf,"* *Anglistica xxv* (Copenhagen: Rosenkilde and Bagger, 1986).

The information on p. xii about the saga copier Magnus Bjornsson comes from Donna Urschel, "The Sagas of Iceland: Symposium on Literature and Icelandic Culture," *Library of Congress Information Bulletin*, July 2000.

Glam's Story

This is based on a famous episode in the *Grettis saga Asmundarsonar*. A number of scholars have argued that the fight — a night battle against a monster who invades a house — is based on an original ur-story that also underlies the story of Beowulf and Grendel. If so, there are significant differences. Beowulf is a noble who later becomes a king. His fight takes place in a king's long hall, and his opponent Grendel is an authentic monster, who has been killing warriors. Grettir is fighting an undead slave in a farmhouse, and Glam has mostly been killing sheep.

I have changed the story some. In the original, Glam is not murdered. He is simply a dead slave, who will not lie quietly in his grave. I have given him a reason for refusing to be dead and made the farm family obnoxious, except for the wife.

My Grettir is not too far off from the saga hero, and I follow the saga exactly when I say that Glam's eyes, shining in the moonlight, make Grettir forever afraid of the dark.

Kormak the Lucky

The story of the slaves killed to hide the silver comes from *Egils saga Skallagrimssonar*. In that, Egil — eighty years old and blind — managed to kill both slaves. I have wanted to save one of the slaves for years and finally managed to do it.

The story of Volund comes from the Eddic poem *Volundarkvitha*. I haven't changed the story, except to give Volund a daughter and make him (maybe) a bit less awful.

If you wonder why Volund becomes grim when he hears "yo-to-ho," that is the call of the Valkyries in Wagner's "Ride of the Valkyries." The reference is way out of period, since Wagner's *Ring* cycle is from the nineteenth century. Still, Wagner's operas and my story draw on the same Norse legends, and I couldn't resist.

The light elves come from Icelandic folklore. The dark elves are briefly mentioned in Snorri Sturlason's *Prose Edda*. We know nothing about them except their name. Everything about them in this story, including their electric trains, has been made up by me.

The Black School

The first two stories in this collection are based on sagas. "The Black School" is based on folktales. Saemundur was a real Icelandic cleric, who studied in mainland Europe, though not at the devil's Black School. He established a center for learning at Oddi and became famous for his wisdom.

While this book was in production, John D. Berry pointed out that the university in Paris was not founded until circa 1150, so Saemundur could not have studied there. I am stuck with Saemundur's dates (1056–1133), and I don't want to rewrite the story. Therefore the mentions of the university have been left in. The story is based on folktales, not history, and the folk often get details wrong. Scholars today believe Saemundur may have studied in Franconia, rather than in France.

In folklore, he is a magician and an opponent of the devil, always (as far as I know) able to outwit the Evil One.

Icelandic trolls are ambiguous, often evil, but sometimes friendly and kind. I lean toward the kind in my stories. If this story has a moral, it's "Don't piss on a troll," or on any working person.

The Puffin Hunter

The elves in this story come from Icelandic folklore.

There are were-animals in the sagas — for example, Kveldulf in the *Egils saga*. As the elves in "Kormak the Lucky" explain, Kveldulf could send his spirit out in wolf form. But I know of no were-animals in Icelandic folktales, and I have never heard of were-birds. However, the world needs them, and puffins are enchanting.

My Husband Stein

The title comes from an Icelandic folktale, "My Husband Jon," which describes how an old farmwife gets her reprobate husband into heaven. I like the title and have used a version of it for a very different story.

The Karahnjukar hydroelectric project is real and has drained most of the water from a famous river. Skyr is also real, a kind of Icelandic yogurt. It has been dyed different colors and thrown at politicians.

The story of Loki and the Apple Corer has been made up by me. ·

BOOK DESIGN AND COMPOSITION by John D. Berry. The text type is Huronia, designed by Ross Mills; the display type is Beorcana, designed by Carl Crossgrove.